Bagz oF money

SLIMCONSIN

I0663765

content

Turn Up For The Streets

by

Blue Hunnid

Turn Up For The Streets

ISBN: 978-1-7366158-6-7

Table of Contents

Chapter One – Keisha

See, they had to start this shit off with me first because it's only right. let me start off by giving y'all a description of myself. I'm 5'9" with honey brown colored skin, brown eyes, shoulder length hair and just the right amount of body to get the job done. Even though I have shoulder length hair, all natural, I still prefer to style my crown with micros or box braids. I'm not gonna sit here and lie and say that I'm all hood because I'm not. I come from an okay life, but I've had my issues along the way. When I was eighteen, I went to the army and that's what put me on the right track. I didn't stay the full ride; I just got in long enough to receive a monthly check for the rest of my life, though. While I was in, I took up culinary arts and business because my dream is to one day own my own restaurant. A dream is only a dream if you sleeping on it. Nowadays, I ain't doing shit, but enjoying life and wilding the fuck out.

I got a thing for thugs. I don't know what it is or why I love a gun toughing, drug dealing, rob a nigga, or bitch, type of nigga, but I do. Especially if he light skinned with them funny color ass eyes. Don't let them muthafuckas know how to change. Oh my God, I can't deal. I like a man with tattoos and fit body, because I'm petite and like to be picked up sometimes. I'm most definitely a freak by nature and an animal from the back. I also like a nigga that can dress and is always fresh every time you see him.

That's why, soon as I saw Yella for the first time, it was like love at first sight. I met Yella through my cousin JC one day when I video called him on Facebook and Yella just so happened to be around.

Actually, my cousin was riding with Yella, and I just so happened to get a glimpse of him when the screen turned his way. When I say I wanted to jump through the phone straight into that nigga lap, that's what I really mean. I played it cool, but at the same time, I made sure that stopping by my house was in their plans before I ended the call.

Long story short, they came and we smoked and chilled and got to know each other. When they pulled up, I was waiting on my front porch in a pair of black Tre Religion jeans and a black True Religion shirt with gold writing that spelled the label across my C-cup titties. On my feet, I had on a pair of black and gold OVO Jordans. I liked wearing twelves, elevens, and thirteens. Don't ask me why because I can't tell you, that's just my swag.

When they pulled up, I noticed that they were in a white Dodge Challenger. I knew the car was a rental because it had a bar code sticker in the window. Regardless of that, they were still chilling, and I liked what I saw so far. They never got out. Instead, I got in and we left out of my neighborhood. I didn't stay in the hood because my military check afforded me the luxury of living on the outskirts of Durham up 70 of on the way toward Raleigh. I lived around mostly white folk and Asian muthafuckas who were nosey as hell and always watching my every move. So, when Yella jacked the music up all loud and shit, it kind of irked my nerves but I ain't say nothing, though. What I did do, was check that nigga out from my vantage point in the backseat. I was liking what I saw, and I had every intention on getting to know Yella with his red sexy ass. I know I was eye candy to him as well because we made eye contact through the rearview mirror. I could tell he liked what he saw, and I was glad because I just had to have a piece or two of him.

We rode around for almost two hours just smoking and listening to Lucci. We stopped a couple times, and I could tell that the stops were drug related. If I had to guess at the time, I would have said that Yella sold crack and I would've been right. We were in East Durham, and I knew the area was notoriously known for its drug traffic and prostitution. After another thirty minutes of the same thing, I was relieved to see that we were pulling into the parking lot of the Big Apple because I was thirsty as hell after having smoked so much loud. As we were backing into a spot near the entrance to the store, I noticed several characters standing around doing them. Some were prostitutes, some were stragglers, and the rest were just straight up hood niggas.

Once the car was in park and Yella hopped out, he was almost immediately surrounded by fiends. I didn't know it at the time, but Yella was the man to see over that way if you wanted that drop. Next, my cousin got out and then let the seat up so I could follow. Once I was freed from my temporary prison, I went straight into the store and grabbed me a pineapple and orange Snapple along with some cool ranch Doritos and a pack of Starburst. Snacks in hand, I made my way towards the counter to pay for my items. Before I could even get there, Yella came strolling through the door counting a small stack of money. From where I stood, I could see that the bills were a mix of fives, tens, twenties, and ones. Definitely block money at its best. I watched as he finished his count and then folded it and stock in in his pocket. He then went into his front right pocket and pulled out yet another stack. Unlike the first one though, this one held the big faces.

"Yo, Ali, let me get a box of chocolate Dutch Master cigarettes, a pack of Newport's, and whatever she getting" Yella said speaking to the store clerk who only smiled as Yella handed him a five dollar bill.

I was in awe as I peeped that nigga swag. He was wearing all white with some baby blue and white Lebron's. He had a big ass Cuban around his neck, a gold Rolly on his left wrist, a gold bust down bracelet on his right, and four big boys' rings, two on each hand. That nigga was shining, and I saw him.

"Thanks, you" was all I could say as we turned to leave after Ali had placed our items in a black plastic bag. Stepping back out into the sun I watched as Yella looked around cautiously before his head stopped moving and his eyes stayed glued to a dark gray charger that had planted itself directly across the street. I knew it was the police because of the dark ass tint and everybody else did to.

"Fuck!" I heard Yella say before he turned to look my way. "You know how to drive?" he asked me as he stared at me with those eyes.

"Yeah, I can drive." I answered.

"Aight, well jump in the driver seat and get us away from here because if Garcia see me get behind the wheel, he gonna act stupid!" Yella said as he made his way to the passenger side of the car.

"Yo, JC come the fuck on before you get left!" Yella added before hopping in and closing the door. He didn't have to say it twice before my cousin came running and jumped in the back.

"Where we going?" I asked as I adjusted my seat and put my seatbelt on before looking his way.

"Shit, hit the highway, we going to Raleigh. You ain't got nothing to do, right?" he asked me while simultaneously keeping an eye on the charger that still sat across the street.

"Nah, I'm all yours!" I said before realizing what my words could mean.

"Oh yeah?" He said with a smirk on his face as he now looked at me.

"You know what I mean!" I said before trying to clean it up just a little bit.

"Yeah. Aight!" Was all he said before he leaned his seat back and then turned the radio up.

Chapter Two – Yella

It was just my luck to pull up in the hood when the fucking Law was out on they bullshit. It wasn't no secret that I was making moves in the east, because the streets talked, and the police listened. I'm not gonna sit here and flex like I'm moving bricks because I ain't never been no fronting ass nigga. I am playing with a nine though and I don't sell n weight all bust down. I fate dealing with niggas but I loving fucking with the fiends though. In a twenty-four-hour period if shit moving good, I might run through three of four ounces worth of dimes and dubs.

Keeping it all the way real, when I'm on the block, can't nobody else eat because I got the best shit and I'm the only nigga that's doing three dimes for the twenty. Not to mention that I don't ever sleep. A muthafucka can call me four in the morning and I'm coming if the number is right. Shit, nine times out of ten, I'm probably already on the block, in the cut, in somebody spot, or backed up in somebody driveway with a walkie talkie to communicate with my runners. I had shit on smash and niggas mad, so I also had to keep a fif with a stick in it.

I got a whip, but I rather ride rental because the police know my shit and every time I pull it out, I get pulled. Muthafuckas know I be having shit, but then can never catch me because I always stay six steps ahead of they ass. If I am dirty out the gate, it's a high speed because I rather take a fleeing to elude or resisting arrest then to get hit with the pole and the work. In my city, nigga like me get caught up with that combination I already know the Feds coming to holla at me and I don't need them problems with them people. That's why I move the way I does because I know I got a target on my back.

I ain't always been in the position I'm in. Shit, when I first started out, I had a half a gram, and I was sleeping in the trap house. Then, like magic I took that half to a whole to two to three point five and I kept flipping until I reached a zip. Once I got to that scansion I ain't never looked back. Now, I'm on my way up and I ain't really tryna come down. I'm copping a nine every three days and I got thirty-nine stack stuck in a lock box up under my mama's house out by South Pointe. I ain't rich, but I'm living and trying to enjoy life. That's why as I sat in the passenger seat of my rental while shorty drove, I was on Facebook flexing with my little money.

I was the fuckin selfie king and everybody knew it. I had about five bands on me, but when you got one's fives, tens, twenties, fifties, and blue faces it made it look like sixty. Plus, my jewelry was shining and that shit alone was worth about another thirty. I ain't walking in no store and pay for it myself, but I know its value from having took it to my man's at Pat's Pawn. I probably gave up maybe an ounce and a half at different times for different pieces. I was the king of finessing as well so that played a part in my rise to the top.

While I was uploading phones and posting shit on my timeline, I had JC in the back rolling up some of that blue cheese kush that had just hit the city. I knew this because my cousins Tay and Darrin were the ones pushing it, and for two fifty, I had been blessed with forth two grams of some shit that you couldn't even smoke a whole blunt of. No sooner than I smelled the smoke in the air, my Galaxy beeped notifying me that I had a text. Looking at it, I laughed because my nigga Bandanna had hit me up asking me what was up not even knowing I was on my way to Raleigh to holla at him. Not bothering to text back, I opted to call instead. The phone rang two times before my nigga's voice came through the car speakers for everybody to hear.

"Yooo!"

"What's goody, my nigga?" I asked as I grabbed the blunt from JC who was passing it to me as he coughed up his longs.

"Shit! just got out the sower! what up with it though?" He talked as a voice in the background yelled his name. It sounded like his girl, Krystal, but knowing that nigga… it could've been any bitch, for real! My nigga was like me in a lot of ways. The only difference between us was that he was dark skinned and short with long dreads, while I was six feet even with short dreads.

"Man, the hood hot as fuck around my way so I'm on my way up the road." I told him already knowing it was welcome without checking. Shit, we did this almost every day. Either he came to Durham or I went to Raleigh. That's just how it was with us. Even though my nigga was a Red I still fucked with him like we was my family. Me and bandanna had met in prison where we were both serving bids at Scotland Correctional in North Carolina. Now, we were both out and on our grind. I slung crack and he liked to bust checks.

"Aight, who you with?" he asked me, but I was already knowing he ain't really care. The question was more of a habit than urge to really know, still, I told him anyways.

"Me, JC, and his cousin!" I said with a smile as I looked over at her as she drove.

"You still got the Challenger or you took it back already?" he asked me and I already knew why. He had the same car, his was just red instead of white like the one I had. I had done mine for almost two weeks, but for almost a month. Brah had the car so long and was dogging it so much that he had to put a new set of tires on the bitch because he had ran them bold.

"Yeah, I got it, but I think I might go get that new Hyundai Genesis tomorrow though cuz it's about time for me to switch it up. You know I gotta stay a step ahead of these muthafuckas out here." I explained as I passed the blunt to Keisha who took it.

"Yeah, I already be knowing! Big fact! But where you at right now?" he asked me as I pointed to the Capitol Boulevard exit for her to take.

"We almost on Capitol! You at the crib, right?" I asked already knowing he was there. Brah stayed behind the Ice plex in some little town house that ran like fifteen hundred a month. Like I said, brah played with them checks and all he wear is True Religion.

"Aight, bet, and yeah I'm at the crib tryna find me some gas."

"Ain't gotta look no more cuz I got some of that real blue cheese on me right now!" I informed him as we made the right by where Doctor Jay's used to be.

"Say less, my nigga!"

"Less said, but we about to pull up in like two seconds, though" I told him as I stuffed my cash back into my pocket and once again took the blunt from JC.

"Facts'" he said before hanging up in my ear. I knew it wasn't disrespect because that just how we did. Like I said that nigga was my brother for real, for real!

Chapter Three - Bandanna

I already knew my nigga was fresh as fuck because I had peeped his Facebook post with the pictures and shit. That wasn't none new because me and him did that shit on a daily basis. I really fucked with brah on another level, and I looked at him like he was my brother. That nigga a whole one hundred and any time I need that nigga he always comes through for me no matter what the situation is. Guns, drugs, bitches, or murder, it didn't matter.

I figured since my nigga had on all white that I was gone follow this lead and do the same. I preferred True's over anything but today I slid into a pair of all white Rodin's with the black and red spikes. I threw on a white polo vee with the red logo and a pair of red, white, and black foam. I wasn't big on jewelry, but I did have a plain Jane rolly on my left arm with a four finger ring that spelled out my name across my knuckle. I had my dreads done and braided to the back with a Chicago Bulls snap facing forward on top of my head as a one carat diamond danced in each of my ears. I knew I was the shit and the stank ass look on my lil ho Krystal's face only confirmed it. The bitch was a world class hater and a fuckin grand champion when it came to cock blocking. Still, I was in love with her white ass and the things she could do with a dick in her mouth. At the moment, she was wifey and all that but at the same time she could be replaced, and she knew it.

"So, where you going looking all like that?" she asked as I put a couple dabs of Polo Red on my neck and wrists. She was talking to me from the California king that I had purchased for the spot when we moved in. She was still naked from me having slid out of her body before my shower.

"Now I know you nosy ass just heard me on the phone with Yella, so why you asking question you already know the answers to?" I asked her right back as I slid my iPhone into my pocked followed by my cash.

"Yeah, I heard you, but I never heard you say anything about a location!" She pointed out. It was times like these when I would rather be single because when a bitch had you committed, they acted as if they were your mother or something!

Shaking my head before I answered, I said "I don't know what we gonna do yet but what's with all the questions?" Before she could answer though I heard music outside followed by horn blowing. I already knew it was brah, so I ain't even have to check.

"Look, I'll be back in a little while so just hit me if you need me. It's a stack in the dresser just in case you need some money." I said making a quick exit before she had a chance to stop the show with more bitching and questions. A nigga was ready to go and get the say started and my ace boon coon was outside waiting.

Walking outside, I saw that brah had backed in right beside my rental so I walked towards that direction, One I got up little closer, that's when I say that Yella was in the passenger seat and some girl was driving. He had already told me who he was with, but old girl was a new face. She was bad and I knew that she was my nigga's type just by looking at her.

"So, what goody?" I asked as I dapped my nigga through the open passenger window. I nodded at JC because I had seen with and around brah a few times, but I didn't know the boy personally. I then nodded at old girl, and she smiled in return.

"Ain't shit my nigga what it is?" Yella asked after we had dapped up.

"What we doing? We getting in traffic or nah?"

"I'm with whatever my nigga I'm just tryna let this sun go down so I can get on my Batman shit ya feel me!" Yella said and I already knew what he was talking about because I had been on the clock with him more than a few times.

"Aight, well, let's go see what up around the way then!" I said as I stepped back and then turned to jump into my own rental! All I really listened to was Money Bagg and Lucci so I plated inny minny miny mo with the two, and came up with Lu!

A few seconds later, I heard my boy coming through the Bose speaker that cam factory with the RT. I had A half of a blunt in the ashtray, so I lit that ho and then I tore out the causing the tires to screech, I looked in the rearview to see if my nigga was behind me and just like I knew, her was!

I already knew I was sliding first because I was straight out the south side and everybody in Raleigh knew it. I came up under Gooch up until he got killed at the barber shop one day by some niggas that were related to a nigga that he got killed! I don't know, I guess he didn't think bra had no niggas riding for him.

Nevertheless, me and the hounds fucked the city up behind that shit. I personally caught two stains and shit bags. My muthafuckin aim was the greatest, so when I came out the window or walk up ain't no missing. If I do its cause of the grace of God. One thing about it through, I'm gonna keep spinning until I get off.

Since I had to go and pick up some cake from my lil homie Finesse I decided to head over to Martin first. I had Finesse in charge of getting random people around to different banks to the checks that I be Printing up and eating off of. My biggest lick was for a hundred thousands, and I only had to do eleven months behind it when I go caught. After that little bd I got smarter and came out and recruited a squad of muthafucka to go bust so mu hands stayed clean. The only thing I was guilty of was possessing the equipment to make it happen. Along with the checks I also played with the swipe game. I kept at least forty to fifty cards on me at all times because they were all loaded. Every time I stopped somewhere that had an ATM machine, I made sure to make that bitch tap out. I wasn't playing with it because I loved to be up I'm trying to win. Big facts!

It didn't take long to get to Matin from where I lived because I knew where I was going and I was doing damn near the dash on every straight away. It was still early, so the law wasn't really out yet. As soon as I turned on the block, I notice that it was already jumping. Fiends everywhere, so I knew that my nigga Yella was about to make a little something. I had been introduced brah to the hood, so his face was already platinum! Once I got to the middle of the block, I pulled over and parked in front of the stop that knew the lil hommie lived in. I didn't even have to blow the horn because Finesse was already outside.

As soon as Finesse saw me park, she came strutting my way looking like a whole snack. She was light brown skinned with long micros and an ass that was nice and high. Finesse had that type of body that made a nigga want to want her just by looking. Shawty was a bad bitch, but we ain't never take it there because she used to be Cooch's bitch before he got whacked. Plus I had shawty directly under me and it just wouldn't have felt right if I fucked my lil hound. I did hook her and Yella up though. I mean shit if I hadn't, the way they were eye fucking each other the first time I introduced them, it would've probably happened anyway.

18

"What's pippin food?" She asked me as she slid into the passenger seat smelling like Gucci Pleasure. She was another True Religion junkie, so I wasn't surprised to see her in it from head to ankle with Jordans on her feet. The bitch had fine chains and I don't know how many bracelets. Everything was gold and bust done compliments of a muthafucka that we didn't even know, all we knew was that the cracker had a couple million in his account, so we cashed out.

"We poppin?" I answered as we did the shake right before she reached into her Birkin and pulled out six thousand dollar stacks. I already knew to be expecting sixty because I had printed sixty different checks for a stack apiece. I didn't have to worry about paying nobody because Finesse did all that for me. She was my middle woman and she has her own middleman that dealt with the busters. Like I said before had taught me a lot and I was way smarter about it now than I was before.

"I hear that shit. I see you got ta boy with you!" She said with a smirk, but I already knew what time it was. She was trying to fish but I couldn't be baited. Not going against my nigga anyway! If he wanted her to something, I knew he would let it b known himself.

"Don't start that bullshit today, Finesse!" I warned sternly as I cut my eyes at her. She already knew how I felt about Yella so she knew to start no shit.

"Whatever! That nigga know better than to roll up in my section with some off brand ass bitch. That nigga gotta be high off that shit he selling." She rated with a mean mug on her face. Shawty was killer for real but deep down she still had feelings like any other bitch.

"Brah, y'all not even together though, and didn't you and that lame O'Brian just start kicking it? You know that streets talk and I heard what it said!" I said as I liked at her and waited on a response.

"Shit, a bitch gotta have fun too!" she fired back laughing in a way that me it sound like a revenge fuck or something.

"Whatever! Y'all ain't no couple anyway and ain't been fuckin that long" I told her as I stuffed the ones she had just given me into a back and gold bag, I kelp everything in that bitch to. Money, weed, and forth with a fifty that spit like a choppa. I always kept it in the backseat for easy access since my seat stayed leaned back.

"Yeah, you right but just a respect thing. Don't be bring nobody where I roam and be at though! Anyway, what y'all about to get into? Know y'all hos ain't up to no good."

"Shit, we chilling! Brah hood hot so he cooling until the sun go down and shift change." I told her as I checked my reflectionn in the rearview. Once I saw everything was nice and tight, I leaned back in my seat and prepared myself to feel out.

"Aight, well shit I'm gong fuck it!!" Finesse said trying it.

"Ah, no the fuck you not! I got a lil ho I'm about to be sliding with today and I don't need no stragglers with me!" I flexed serious as hell.

"Oh word? Aight, that cool! I hope your dick fall off nigga." she shot back and then reached for the door to exit.

"And if it do, I'm gonna buy me another one! " I said before she closed the door. Shit, I wasn't trying to be fucking with Finesse.

I had other shit to do and lil bitch I met two days before was trying to chill. I was just coming out of Saxby's when I had bumped into the baddest bitch I seen in Raleigh in a long time. That lil bitch was like that, and today was the day I was gonna get a chance to vibe with her. So, as I pulled out, I got to the car and made it call her.

Chapter Four - Yella

As soon as we turned onto Marth, I already knew where this nigga was going. I knew he was probably going to pick up some chicken from Finesse's crazy ass. Me and old girl fucked a couple times, but it wasn't noting like that. She already knew what it was with me from the jump. See, I wasn't one of them niggas that told a bitch what she wanted to hear. Instead, I told her the truth so that I wouldn't have to deal with all that arguing bullshit. The way my temper is set up, I can't be doing no back and forth because I have a short fuse. I wasn't no woman better but I'd slap the shit outta ho, though.

As we pulled down, I noticed how the strip was jumping and I knew off top that I was about to make a lil bit of quick change. Once we parked and shit, I saw how Finesse eyed me through the windshield as she made her way up to Bandanna's rental. I knew her ass was 38 just by the way she was looking. Still, I wasn't thinking of Finesse right then though because I had fresh fish on the line.

The fiends on this block knew my face because my nigga had put me out there already. Plus, once they got a taste of the product I had to offer, it was a wrap every time I came around. I was the best when it came to cooking the work and I had learned the recipe from one of my best runners. Peewee had shown me the way and I had been a fool with it ever since. So as Bandanna conducted his business with Finesse, I stepped out and made a few hand-to-hands. I made about $500 in about five minutes, but I still would've preferred to have been on my own block. It was all good because I had left Auntie Fran with a lil something so I knew for a fact that I wouldn't miss much.

As soon as I saw the passenger door open on Bandana's rental, I hurried up and jumped back in mine so I wouldn't hear no fuck shit from Finesse. Baby girl was cool and all, but I wasn't really looking for no relationship with her. Lucky for me, she didn't even bother to look in my direction. I wasn't sweating it, though, because the way I had her yelling the last time we fucked I knew she'd let me right the fuck in.

Leaning back after I grabbed the blue cheese from the center console, I proceeded to pull out two big buds so I could break em down, roll em up, and smoke it. I was a real pothead, but I fucked with the pills and drank as well. I ain't no addict or nothing I just get faded now and then.

Once I rolled out the blunt, I looked over at old girl and just really looked at her like for real. The whole time we had been riding she hadn't said anything or asked shit, I ain't really know how to take her but I was about to pick her brain though.

"So, you always drive niggas' cars you don't even know? Or is this just some random shit that happens in life sometimes?" I asked her as my eyes stayed trained on her body for any type of reaction.

"This is just some random shit!" she answered smiling taking a quick glance at me. Once she looked back toward the road, I did as well, and I saw that we were creeping up New Bern Avenue near the car wash. We were headed to the barbershop. On top of that, there was a tattoo shop right next to it, a clothing store on the other side, and a restaurant right beside that, so this little strip stayed jumping. More than once, when I had been through Raleigh, I witnessed niggas coming through on bikes and also riding foreign.

"So that was your spot where we got you from?" I asked her as I also passed her the blunt.

"Yeah!" she answered quickly before taking a strong pull. She immediately started choking, so I reached over and patted her on the back.

"Thank you" she said.

"You good, but what's up with you? Where your little man at?" I asked, to see if she is fucking with a nigga or nah. I really ain't give a fuck but it as just good to know.

"I ain't got no man but I'm looking for one" she said all sexy to me while giving me that look!

Shit the way was acting I knew that I was about to be in that pussy real soon. I really ain't say nothing to her until we got to the strip. Just like I said we pulled up to the barbershop and it was jumping. We barely had a place to park out that bitch. Lucky for us a big boy dodge ram truck sitting on thirties was just pulling off and it opened enough space to squeeze us both in since I knew that Bandanna's big homie had gotten smoked at this same barbershop, I made sure to grab my F&N 57. I wasn't trying to go out bullshitting, and I damn sure knew I wasn't going for getting bodied in another city. As soon as we jumped out, my nigga started his bullshit. He was always extra with it but that's why we clicked because we both was.

"Damn where you get her from my nigga? How you doing, baby? My name Bandanna, aka Bando, aka Bands, if you really know me!" He said asking me and greeting her at the same time. I didn't even bother to answer but she did.

"I'm fine and the name is Keisha!" she said while smiling sweetly.

"Aight, Keisha well you in my city so everything on me. It don't matter what it is, if you want it just let me know!" Bandanna said.

"Well, why ain't the weed on you then nigga?" I asked jokingly, causing the four of us to all laugh.

"You ain't said shit, I'll pay for that lil bit of tree you got!" he offered as he pulled a couple bands out his pocket. He knew that I as just fucking with him, but he just wanted to show off anyway.

"Nah, it's good, it's on me, fam!" I told him as we continued to step toward the action.

As we made our way to the door, we passed by several different whips ranging from Chargers to Benzes, Infinities, different trucks, and a few top of the line foreigns I knew cost like a quarter mil. See in Raleigh the drug game was jumping, but most niggas was getting they cheese off that bunk shit. Them niggas was for real with it and really eating off that shit. My nigga Bands was a prime example.

As we got to the front, I saw a nigga that I had been in a group home with when I was like 14 years old. I ain't know what he was on, so I gripped! I guess he was still on the porch though, because he gave me a nervous smile and tried to dap me the fuck up like we was cool. Last I had checked, we was beefing so I was tryna keep it hot.

"Nah, nigga, we ain't like that, what up?" I asked, ready to fire.

Shit, how I was thinking I was out of town so wasn't nobody gonna know but us. Shit worse come to worse I'd just nod the bitch and her cousin on my way back to Durham I already knew Bandanna wasn't gonna be a problem because he was a whole one hundred.

"Yo, what's good? You know Bruh?" Bands asked me as he looked at my face and then down to where my hand was.

"Yeah, I know him, we to be in a group home back in the day!" I told him as I continued to mug that fuck nigga.

I smelled the fear coming out that nigga's pores! He looked about ready to run but I had too many shots to miss.

"Man, that shit was when we was kids, bruh, we grown now!" He stated, trying to reason with me.

"Man, fuck that shit my nigga, we chillin and you supposed to be ducked off anyway. Let that shit go bruh." Bands told me.

I looked at him and then I looked at old buddy. Old girl and JC hadn't said shit at all. They was just looking and waiting to see what I was gonna do.

"Yeah, you right!" I said relaxing and letting my hand fall to my side. I was on some more shit, but I held grudges.

"Bruh, go head be bout your business though we up!" Bands told old boy as he start to step again.

Falling in line, I watched that nigga out my side view just to make sure he wasn't trying to do some dumb movie shit and spin around on his ass.

"I'm glad you ain't do nothing to that boy." Keisha told me, as she looped her arm through mine as she walked beside me.

"Yeah, I wanted to trip but it's all good! What up though? You hungry? They got the best chicken and shrimp in Raleigh right here!" I said as we walked through the door of Too Much Flavor.

I knew the whole menu by heart because I done had everything they had.

"Yeah, I can eat something. They got fries right?" she asked me.

We were at the counter now because luckily there wasn't a line. "Yeah, they got fries!" I answered laughingly.

It didn't take us long to get our food. After we ate and I ordered some wings to go, we went next door to the barbershop. The barbershop wasn't no ordinary spot though, because it really went down in that bitch. Niggas were always betting on games and just like any other time, the sports tv was on a game. That wasn't the only thing that they were betting on though, because they also had two game systems set up. Madden, NBA2K or Call of Duty could get you paid if you was like that. I hadn't ever tried my luck but Bands had. I watched him with a couple bands one day playing Madden. He fucked around and skunked a nigga and made him have to kick out double.

"What's good, Bando?" the owner asked as he looked just like Yo Gotti on some real shit and he liked to wear a neck full of chains that gave up a light show every time the light hit off his neck.

"Ain't shit just peepin the scene my nigga, how you?" Bandanna asked dapped him up.

"Oh aight, I'm good though. I see you got your boy with you. What's up, fam?" He spoke to me because he knew my face from having come through before.

"It's all love, my nigga, I'm just tryin to live. Ya feel me?" I replied to him.

I ain't go dap him like Bando did but he knew what it was.

"Shit, I just got came to check you out my nigga! We bout to get up out of here though. I'll catch you later on bro!" Bandanna said.

It wasn't really too much going except the usual. All the action was outside in the front. As son s we stepped back out of the door we saw like twenty bikes fly by doing the dash. They was out there cutting up and the hoes was cheering like little groupies or some shit. I mean them hos was out there too. You know how that shit go when it's money around. Hos gonna be hos because they trying to get chose. It was the middle of August, so it was still hot out. In another month or two the summer heat would be gone and the cold air would be moving in.

Looking at my watch, I saw that it was going on 1 o'clock. I had five more hours until shift change. I knew the po-pos' schedule by heart. They changed out at six and the new unit was on duty by 6:30. Every day was the same thing unless it was the DT's. them bitches worked from 8-6, Monday-Friday and did random busts on Saturdays and Sundays.

Hearing my favorite song by Lucci plying off my phone, I knew that somebody was trying to reach me. Reaching into my pocket and retrieving it, I looked at the screen to see who it was. I knew the number, but I didn't have it saved which told me it was a play calling. That's just how I did. The only way I would save a number is if it didn't have anything to do with my illegal dealings.

"Yeah, who's this?" I asked answering my jack.

I knew it was money, but I wasn't in the city, so it had to be about something to make me move.

"Hey baby boy, this Peewee! Where you at? Boy, this bitch is jumping out here and your Aunt Fran said she out!"

See, Peewee was one of my runners, but he was also family to me on my daddy's side. I could tell that nigga to do anything and it would get done, no questions asked.

"Oh yeah? What the police doing?

"Because last I saw, the fucking task force was out there."

"Man, them bitches ain't on shit, they riding, though. That's how they always do, you know that!" He said trying to convince me.

He ain't have to though because I knew if he was calling then everything was everything.

"What about Garcia and Finesse?" I asked trying to see if anyone of them was out there.

Both of them bitches hated me, and the feeling was mutual because they were always trying to stop my show. Finesse had gotten my big brother Edward a seven to ten-year sentence, and Garcia was just a bitch ass nigga. He as always on his bullshit trying to pull me or jumping out on me at the store. The problem was, I was to fucking smart for the bullshit and I was always ready at any time.

"Man, nephew if I'm calling, you know what it is! Where you at? Pull up before you fuck around and miss all this money and let these little fuck niggas get it all." He replied.

"WHAT NIGGAS?"I asked heated because muthafuckas knew I didn't play that shit.

"Man, Muffin done brought some clowns over here from North Durham somewhere and they got straight garbage" he told me.

I had to laugh because I wanted to know how he knew all that. You know how fiends do though, so I guess he had hit something that somebody had got from them. Wasn't no crack head turning down no free crack. I don't care how good or bad it is or how much they already had themselves.

"Aight, Peewee, I'm on my way!" I said ready to hang up and hit the highway.

"How long you gonna be?" Peewee asked.

I knew he was fishing so he would know what to tell everybody that he probably had waiting.

"I'm coming down 70 now, leaving Raleigh!" I lied like I usually did.

I never told a muthafucka no specific time. If I knew it would be an hour, I would tell them thirty minutes. If I knew I would be twenty minutes, then I'd tell them ten.

"Aight, well hurry up nephew it's money out here" he replied before I hung up.

Wasn't shit else that needed to be said though, he already convinced me to slide back to the hood. I guess my nigga already knew what time it was because he was looking my way. I guess he heard my side of the conversation.

"You about to slide, bruh?" Bandanna asked me.

"Yeah, I gotta get back!" I told him as I went into my back pocket and threw him the fourteen grams of blue cheese that I has already made up my mind to give him.

"I'm gonna get with you later, fam, hit my line!" I said as I dapped him up and turned to leave. I heard Keisha and JC behind me saying bye and a minute later we were all back in the car. This time, I was driving because I had to push it to go ahead and get back to the block.

Chapter Five

Peewee looked at the phone and smiled because he knew his nephew as on the way and that meant free crack for him. Peewee wasn't the average crack head though. He wasn't like the street walkers and the muthafuckas that basically lived on the block. He had a wife, a crib, and he cut hair. On the weekends though, he turned into Pooky and went stupid. Peewee had been around for a long time though. He had seen it all and smoked even more.

"What my baby say?" Fran asked him once he gotten off the phone.

She was standing across the street talking to another fiend that went by the name CeeCee. CeeCee was a smoker too, but she could've been a model if she hadn't let crack take over her world. She was a redbone with a phat ass and she looked like she could be Lisa Raye's little sister.

"Nephew coming, he said he coming down 70 now" Peewee informed her, causing her to smile.

"Yeah, bitches, my baby coming, my baby coming." She said excitedly as she did a little dance with her stem in one hand and her lighter in the other.

Fran was kind of heavy set with some huge ass titties that were damn near about to jump out of her shirt as she did her little fucked up two step. No matter how much them shits moved though, the twelve hundred dollars that she had stashed in them would stay secure. She had sold every bit of the work Yella had left her and the rest she smoked.

"Yes, sir I'm glad because this shit is staring at me. Shit won't even met down, done fucked my stem up yo!"Porsha said seriously, as she examined her stem.

Porsha was another regular on the block. She was notoriously known for whooping a bitch or nigga if they slept on her.

"Muffin the one got these fools over here with that boop boop doo doo!" Forest, another regular said.

Forest was one of them muthafuckas that like to joke and play a lot. He was a young smoker and the little bitch ginger that stood beside him was even younger. She had just turned seventeen, but she was already gone off the caine. She was Muffin's little protégé but right then she wasn't feeling her girl at all because she hated bad crack.

"Hope y'all know Yella gonna flip when he roll up!" she said.

Mad wishing he had waited to spend her $40 with Yella.

"Sure is" Fran added looking over at Muffin and the two outsiders that she had with her.

More than likely one or both had tricked with her and she had probably talked them into coming with her to the hood. Word on the street was that Muffin had the best head in East Durham.

"Man, Yella ain't nobody. He don't own this block!" Muffin fired back.

Knowing damn well that when Yella pulled up it was gonna be some shit. She really didn't care, she was just trying to get high and milk the two out of everything she could get. Everybody knew what was up except for the two dudes who continued to stand around and make plays as if they belonged there.

"Shit, that boy and his brother's is royalty around here so stop capping!" Peewee said laughing as he watched a police car go up Holloway Street.

They were all standing on the corner, but Briggs was where most of the action was. Briggs and Holloway did number's 24/7 for 365. Then there was Briggs and Lathrop and Guthrie, Park and Lathrop, and anything in between. If you had that fire, you could get money from the BP on Holloway all the way up to the Budget Inn by Wellington Village. All a nigga had to do was keep spinning in a circle all day and he was bound to make and scrape up plenty cake.

As everybody stood around, more and more fiends started to walk up as cars continuously spent the block. Most of the vehicles belonged to tricks who were trying to score some sex and the rest were muthafuckas pulling up to cop. It was a nonstop thing and it always looked like the Carter every second of the day or night.

Peewee was just about to walk into the Blue store that sat on the corner of Briggs and Holloway, when a new Benz truck bent the corner and stopped. When the window came down, an older white man stuck his head out and motioned for Fran to jump in. She didn't even know the man, but they never did. It wasn't nothing for a prostitute to jump in a car they never saw before because it was all about the crack.

"I'll be back, Peewee! Tell Yella I said do not go no damn where until I get back!" Fran said before she hurried up and jumped into the truck.

Just by the way the truck looked he knew that she had just hit the jackpot.

"See if he trying to rent that!" Mils hollered, while standing with the rest of the crowd.

Mils was a young boy that Yella had taken a liking to. He looked just like Kodak Black but he was a good lil nigga.

"Boy, you know she about to get that for Yella." Peewee said knowingly.

He knew Yella was gonna be trying to push that. they did this hit on the regular. Fran or one of the others would fuck the customers socks off and milk them until they were broke. If they had a nice car, then they would talk the customer into renting it out for crack.

"Yeah, I know! I hope he let me push the Challenger then!" Mils said, hoping that Yella would let him stunt in the rental.

Mils wasn't really doing nothing on the block. He was one of them eight ball seven gram type of nigga's that couldn't get over the hump. His problem was that he spent his money faster than he made it and that caused him to fall off every other day No matter how many times Yella had him work or had sent money his way, it didn't matter because Mils couldn't seem to see the bigger picture.

"Look at this bitch!" Peewee said pointing up the block, as he smirked.

Walking towards them was a skinny chick in some baggy ass clothes. Her name was Boosie, and she was also a regular on the block. She looked like death on two legs, but she was a go getter though.

"Oh-kayyy why he got a Jesus piece? He don't even believe in Jesus!" She sang fucking Kodak's song by mixing up the words.

She had a can of beer in a paper bag in her left hand and a stem in the other.

"Girl, what you doing? You got some crack?" Peewee asked her hoping she had some fire on her.

He needed a hit bad, and Yella was taking too long.

"Nope, I'm waiting on Yella!" She replied as she reached the corner and then placed her drink on the ground.

Next, she went into her pocket and pulled out a crispy new one hundred dollar bill.

"You talked to him?" Peewee asked eagerly as he eyed the money.

He was thinking about taking it, but he didn't want Yella to flip on him.

"Yep, he said he about to pull up. Matter of fact, there he go right there." She said pointing before she reached down and picked up her beer and then made her way over to where he was parking on Briggs.

"Yes, sir it's on now, let's get it!"PeeWee hollered as he followed Boosie over to the car.

CeeCee, Forest, Porsha, Ginger, and five other fiends all followed suit so that they could get right. They didn't even have to question if Yella had some good shit because he always did. Muffin didn't even bother to move because she knew that she was about to be on the shit list for the day. She knew that Yella was about to flip but she just prayed that he didn't get to shooting and doing nothing crazy. Lord knows it blew her high every time she heard the sound of gunfire.

Chapter Six - Yella

As soon as I bent the corner, I saw the two nigga's that Peewee had told me about. I really wasn't in the mood for the bullshit, and I didn't want to make the block hot, so I had already decided to give them chance to bounce. After that wouldn't be no talking. Aside from them two, I noticed all the regular faces that roamed the block. I had just hung up the phone with Boosie, so I knew I at least had a hundred waiting on me plus what Fran had for me. That's when I realized Fran wasn't on the scene, but I figured she must have been busting a play or something. Before I could even get my shit right to step out, Boosie was already opening my door.

"Goddamn, Boosie!" I fumed.

Sliding out, I placed my strap in my back pocket for easy access.

"Back up, Boosie, damn! Let the man get out first!" Peewee scolded as and the rest stood nearby.

"Fuck it, what's up with it? What y'all need?" I asked pulling out my bag of work.

I had like thirty two grams in a sandwich bag. I ain't ever bag shit up because it took too much time. It was easier for me to just break shit straight off the cookie and it was one less charge I would have to deal with if I ever got knocked off.

"I got a hundred!" Boosie said said excitedly as he handed it to me. I gave her fifteen dimes for that and then I served everybody else one by one until I had blessed the whole strip. Just that quick I had made four and some change.

"I know you got a Scooby snack for me!" Peewee said with his hand out as if he knew he was getting something.

I had them muthafuckas spoiled as shit and it was my own fault. It was all good though because without them I wouldn't be shit. I guess that why they fucked with me too hard because I treat them like human. I never turned my nose up like I was better than them. you don't need a team when you got the fiends. After I handed Peewee two big ass dimes, I put my shit back up and then made my way over to where Muffin was. JC and his cousin were still sitting in the car smoking, but they were gonna have to get out because as soon as Fran got back, I was going inside the spot. Fran had a little crib right behind the store and that was my little trap spot.

"Muffin, what the fuck you got going on?" I asked her calmly as I eyed the two nigga's she had on my block.

They eyed me back curiously and I understood because they didn't know who the fuck I was. They were about to find out, though.

"I ain't got nothing going on, Yella! Don't start that shit!" She replied with a slight attitude.

"Bitch, what the fuck I tell you about bringing muthafuckas over here? This my shit, so nothing move over here unless I give the okay!" I flexed before turning to face the two niggas.

"Now look,I don't know y'all and y'all definitely don't know me. I'm gonna tell you like this, this my block right here bruh. I'm the reason this shit moving like this and I ain't about to see nobody else eating off my blood, sweat, and tears! I'll die for this block! What you gonna do for it?" I asked them fuck niggas after I had stated my cause.

It really wasn't up for discussion though. They had to go or I was blowin! So out the gate, I whipped out. When them niggas saw that pole, they took off on God I ain't lying! It got me to laugh for a little minute. The strip was long and the street wide it's a little bit of a run to be trying to be Jesse Owens. I had to up on them niggas just cause man. Fuck y'all running for!

I only sent like six at them niggas because I wasn't trying to waste my shells. Shit was real and I had beef with the other side. It was on sight with them Hyde Park niggas because we had been beefing off and on behind the very same block that I stood on.

"Dumb ass niggas!" I said shaking my head as I slid my fire back in my pocket.

When I turned back around, Muffin was looking at me with a mug on her face.

"You owe me a hit, bitch!" she told me like that.

I wasn't giving her ass shit. Bitch was lucky I ain't send nothing at her dumb ass too.

"Yeah, aight! You better catch a play and come with it!' I told her as I saw a banging ass white Benz truck pull up and park at the store. I knew it was that new thang because I wanted one.

"There go Fran right there Yella!"PeeWee hollered as I walked back towards the rental.

"Oh yeah? Who she with?" I asked after realizing that Fran was the one that had pulled up in the truck.

"Some cracker!" Peewee replied.

"Shit, I need to get that!" I said already plotting.

I was hoping Fran had already put it in play for me. Once I got to the rental, I stuck my head in the window to holla at JC. I wanted him to take his cousin home because it was time to get to the money. I didn't need her all in my way and shit just in case shit got wicked.

"Yo go drop ya cousin off and come back for me!" I told him before I turned to her.

"Yo I'm gonna hit your line in a lil while after I handle my business!" I explained to her with a slight smirk.

She smiled at me then nodded. I liked this bitch because she was with whatever I said. I needed a bitch like that who listened instead of giving a nigga all that tongue. Once thy pulled off I stepped over to the store where everybody else was. I wanted to see what the fuck Fran had going on. I was trying to be seen in that Benz and I was willing to give that cracker whatever to push it. He even had some rims on that bitch and I already knew the factory system was like that. Once I made it to the truck, Fran stuck her head out of the passenger window with a big ass smile on her face. As soon as I saw it, I knew it was gonna be a good night.

"Get in, nephew! Come on!" she said excitedly making me smile like a little kid.

I did exactly what she told me. Once I got in, I looked around that bitch and inhaled that new car smell. That shit had peanut butter leather everywhere with little bit of woodgrain. the cracker in the driver seat was dressed in khakis and a polo shirt. I couldn't see his feet, but my best guess was that he had on dress shoes or something.

looking at him closer, it looked like I had seen him before somewhere. Before I could ponder about it any further, Fran turned around in her seat and gave me the run down.

"Baby, I already know you want this truck. Well, my friend here can't get any more money off his card until twelve but he trying to get high. He said he not trying to be in the trap so you going to have to get me a room, so we have somewhere to sit, and he said he charging a dime for every hour!" She explained to me while still smiling.

"When he gonna want the truck back?" I asked raising my eyebrow as I looked at him for an answer.

"How long you staying with me, baby?" Fran asked turning from me to look at him.

"Well, I don't know it depends on what you got for me!" He replied looking at me through the rearview.

He was high as fuck and his eyes told me that because of how big they were. I knew what to do for him though, so I went in my bag and broke off a piece. I had to eyeball it because I ain't have no scale but I knew it was either a ball or close to it. I gave it to him and his eyes lit up like a fucking Christmas tree.

"And you gonna get the room as well, right?" He asked me as he handed everything that I had just given him to Fran.

"Yeah, I'm gonna get it. When you ready now?" I asked ready to get them somewhere they were going so I could go about my business.

"Two days?" He said looking back at me with his eyebrow raised.

I was guessing he was asking so I responded.

"Yeah, I can get it for two days. Where y'all trying to go?" I wanted to know so we could go ahead and get there.

"We are going to Carolina Duke!" Fran said getting back into the conversation.

She knew I didn't like to talk too much, so she was playing her position to the fullest.

That's why she was my favorite because she was a real soldier.

"Well, let's go then!" I said as I pulled out my phone to text JC.

I needed him to bring the challenger to Fran's room so I could park it there. Once I did that, I rolled my window down and called Mills over to the truck.

"Yo, hold this and keep it going for me while I take care of them!" I told him as I handed him like ten grams out of my bag.

I was down to fourteen, so I knew I would have to stop by my own room to grab some more work. I needed to put some of the money I had on me up anyway, so it was a win-win. Plus, I knew it would be dark soon, so I needed to change into some black clothing so I could blend in with the night.

Once I had set Mills straight, we backed out of the store and then bent a right on Holloway. Fifteen minutes later, we were pulling up to the hotel. I sent Fran in to pay for the room while me and the cracker stayed in the truck. Once I got them situated and made sure I got my money from Fran, I peeked out and jumped back on the highway headed to 15-501. I was living out of a room at the extended Stay on Tower Boulevard. I had my personal car parked out there so it wouldn't be seen in the hood.

It took me another twenty minutes to get there and another three to get out and run up to the third floor. Sliding my door key into the slot, I watched as the light by the doorknob turned from red to green. As soon as I walked in, I laid my eyes on my main bitch Shannon as she stood in the middle of the floor with water dripping from her body.

Chapter Seven - Shannon

The story should have started with me but that's okay. My name is Shannon and I'm twenty-nine. I'm short and dark skinned with shoulder length hair and an average body. I'm not ugly but I know that I'm not the baddest bitch in the world either. I ain't never had no complaints though, so whatever. Anyway, Yella and I were supposed to be a couple, but you know how niggas do when they start getting a little money. They always forget the bitch that was down with them before the shine.

I had been hearing little gossip here and there about my man but ain't nobody have no proof. Even if they did though, I probably still wasn't gonna leave my nigga. Shit, we done been through way too much for me to let another hoe have what I got. That didn't mean that I wasn't gonna talk shit and show my ass about it. I'm cool, calm, and collect, but I can get stupid as well. Especially when it comes to Yella, because I'm in love and ain't no faking that. I just wish his ass wouldn't stay out in them streets so fucking much. I knew he had to go get it, but damn.

For the past seven months, we had been living out of hotels because Yella was paranoid as hell. I knew it wasn't for nothing though, because the police was always fucking with him. I had to take a couple charges just so Yella wouldn't get sent up the road. We had gotten pulled one night in a crack rental and the police ended up finding twenty five grams of soft, some pills, and two and a half grams of crack. Not to mention the fact that the crackhead had played us and reported the fucking car stolen. A couple weeks after that, the same crackhead had been found on a side street with hr whole head blown off. I ain"t saying that Yella did it, but I know he did, though.

Yella got a real bad temper, and he almost always turns violent when he get mad. That's my baby and I love him. He takes care of me and anything I need or want, I always get. I also have a son, his name is Pooh, but he stays with my mother though. His daddy ain't shit but fuck him because Yella does everything that he can to make sure me and mineis straight. I haven't worked in forever because I ain't got to. All I do is stay in the room most of the time watching TV or stalking Yella's Facebook page. I got rings bracelets, and plenty of clothes because every time Yella buys an outfit or some shoes, he buys me something too. I love that nigga! that's why when I came out of the shower and saw him coming through the door, it made me smile. It was still early so I knew he wasn't gonna be there long. He was probably coming to change his clothes or something.

"Hey, bae!" I sang as I walked up and pressed my wet naked body against him.

The look in my eyes told him that I wanted him.

"What's up?" He asked as I dropped to my knees and freed his dick from where it was.

Without saying a word, I took him in my mouth and showed him why I was his wifey. Up and down and around the head I licked while II stroked his shaft until it was fully erect. Once I had him where I wanted him, I led him over to the bed almost causing him to trip over his jeans that were around his ankles. Once we made it there I got on the bed and bent over before scooting back to the edge. He obviously knew what I wanted because a second later I felt him entering me. I swear this nigga knew how to hit it just the right way because I always came within minutes every time we fucked. Once he got it in good, he started to speed up his pace as I threw it back at him. My pussy was so wet, that you could hear the juices making loud squishing sounds every time he went in or out of me.

"Mmhm, you like that shit, don't you?" he asked me as he slapped my right ass cheek.

He knew I liked to be spanked while I was getting the business.

"Yes, daddy! Please, don't stop hitting my spot!" I told him as I continued to throw that shit back.

I didn't even care that he was up in my stomach. All I cared about was getting my shit off and pleasing my man.

"Shut up! Who pussy is this? Huh?" He asked me as me put one foot on the bed and started to fuck the shit outta me.

He was going in hard and fast, and that shit felt like heaven, I swear. I was still throwing it to him but now I was also rubbing my clit with my finger really fast.

"Oh shit, it's your pussy, daddy!" I screamed while I came again.

I hated Yella's stupid ass for fucking me so good. Shit! That muthafucka would die before I let another bitch have this.

"Tell me anything!" He shot back as he continued to fuck me like a porn star.

I was loving it too because it had been like three days since the last time we fucked.

"Shit, shit, shit oh my God, fuck me I'm about to cum again bae!" I hollered as I felt myself about to nut again.

"Yeah, cum on this dick!" He said as he fucked me like a jackrabbit.

That's how I knew he was about to bust so I started throwing it back harder and faster so I could get my protein for the day. I felt his grip get tighter on my waist and then I felt his nut hitting my walls as his body went limp. He was still pumping but I knew his energy was drained when he slid out of me and plopped down on the bed out of breath. Going into the bathroom, I got a soapy rag and came back out to clean up my mess. Once I had cleaned his dick and his balls, I jumped back in the shower to clean myself off again. By the time I came back out, Yella had changed clothes and was looking inside his white Gucci bookbag. I knew that he had to be getting some work because that's where he kept it. I also noticed a pile of money on the bed, so I went over and started counting it. I always counted his money because that was my job. We already had close to ten thousand in a cereal box located in the cabinet, so I knew to add this to the stash.

"Yo, did old buddy ever come through here?" I heard Yella asking me, so I looked up to see him looking at me.

"Old buddy who?" I asked in return because I didn't know who he was talking about.

Then I remembered that I had sold some dude two guns for him.

"Oh yeah, he came, I already put the money up!" I explained and then went back to counting. See when Yella was gone, he usually sent some of his traps to me because some of his customers didn't like going to the hood. The hotel we stayed in was on a low key side of town, so it was easier to get them to come there rather than convincing them to drive to the trenches.

"Aight, well I'm about to dip! I gotta get back to the hod, You good right?" He asked me as he threw a black V-neck T-shirt over his head. He was wearing black from head to toe, but he still had his jewelry on.

After he slip some money, his phone, gun, and his work into his pockets, he came over to me and kissed me on the lips. I didn't want to see him leave but I knew nothing I said would make him stay. It was what it was.

Chapter Eight - Yella

After I left the hotel and was back in traffic, I hit JC up to see where he was. Once I found out that he was parked in front of Fran's room waiting on me, I hung up. I was doing like ninety on the way back down the highway. the Benz was fast, and it rode smooth as hit no matter how big of a bump I hit. I was in love with that muthafucka but I knew I had to get my bread up all the way before I could go get my own shit. I could've copped something new but then I would have to start from the bottom, and it didn't make sense to be riding big and broke. The two didn't mix so I was gonna keep doing me until could do better.

Once I made back to the Carolina Duke, I scooped up JC and then slid back to the hood. I was coming down Lathrop Street when I saw Shadai and Peewee walking up the street. Shadai was another one of my fiends. She was black as hell with a stupid phat ass that jiggled every time she moved. That ass was dumb soft too. I knew that because I had fucked her like two times. She had a thing for me, so she had given me that pussy. Don't get it fucked up though because I ain't pay for shit it was just a fuck thing. as soon as Peewee saw the truck coming, he hurried up and flagged me down, so I pulled up on them.

"What's up, fool?" I asked after I had dropped the window.

Shadai looking at me but if it wasn't about business, I wasn't fucking with her. We fucked but it wasn't nothing like that. It really happened on some late night shit when I had been on them pills. I fucked her and CeeCee at the same one time. I never paid for shit.

I didn't even give them crack, it was just off of the love they had for a real nigga.

"Ain't shit, nephew. Baby girl just trying to spend and she ain't know ya new number." Peewee explained as Shadai handed me three twenties.

I served her as I sat in the middle of the street. That's just how it was in my hood. It was really going down on the side streets. It was money to be made and I was trying to get it.

"Aight, yo!" I said beeping the horn as I slid off.

Busting a left on Briggs, I pulled straight up on Mills as he was making a play. When he was done, I hit the locks so he could jump in.

"Ey, yo that nigga Ruga been coming through here. Him and nigga Joog riding together in that lil black Ack." Mils told me as he passed me what he had made.

I thumbed through the money as we sat parked on the side of Briggs. It added up to six hundred and fifty-three dollars, so I knew he had maybe one or two grams left. Maybe three at the most because it was three for twenty on my block, I was giving away something that could've been profit but it made me flip faster in the long run. My number game was crazy and I had broken the science down to the nitty gritty. Wasn't nothing like breaking it all down. Crumbs brought fiends and that weight brought the fucking Feds!

"Oh yeah? What he talking about?" I asked wanting to know because I didn't fuck with them Hyde Park niggas.

Me and that nigga Ruga had traded shots on a couple occasions, but nobody ever got hit. That nigga was my biggest fan and he stayed hating because I had shit sown up.

"He ain't stopped yet! He just slid through looking and shit!" Mils explained as he lit a Newport in the backseat.

"How long you got the truck thought?" He asked changing the subject.

"I got this bitch for two days but I'm hoping Fran make something shake for a nigga!" I told him as I pulled off and slid up to the store so I could back in. As soon as I did Forest, CeeCee and ginger all walked up to my side so they could holler at me. Altogether they had forty dollars so gave them six dimes.

"You gonna be out here tonight, right?" Ginger asked me as she started to load her stem up right there beside the truck.

That's just how it went in east Durham. IT WENT DOWN!

"That ain't no question! You already know we bout to make this bitch do the Wytunchi! Y'all just watch my back like I watch y'alls!" I said and then pulled off making a right then a quick left onto Holloway.

There was another store like fifty yards away from the blue store and it stayed packed with traffic too. so everyday all the nigga's who was doing something in the hood would eventually meet at least one time a day there by accident. It was just that timing had nigga's pulling up at the same time.

Just like before I pulled up and backed in. I had already spotted Tez's car Splash's car, and this nigga Rontay, my fucking brother who was one of them niggas you couldn't depend on if it was life or death. You know how some niggas will set they own bro up to get smoked for some paper? Rontay was one of them!

Niggas didn't even know that it was me in the Benz and I liked it like that because I wanted to make they as sweat for a minute. If someone was about to pull off, I knew that shit was on pause until they saw a muthafucka jump out this bitch. I was cracking up because I could see them breaking they necks to see something. They couldn't see through, because the truck was tinted all the way around. It looked like the Benz had on a pair of sunshades because the windshield was tinted too.

I saw Rontay posted up talking to Splash and Tez as if they were cool like that. Tez was the nigga that was supplying me before I got my weight up and my order got too big for him to fill. I came home and ran it up and pushed everybody to the side. they couldn't out hustle me because I was good at it. The nigga Splash was from Creedmoor but he had fucked round and pulled my lil bitch Brooke and Shay, while I was locked up. The bitch gave that nigga my recipe and he took off. Her little dumb ass was sitting in the passenger seat of his black Infiniti. It was a coupe, but it wasn't up to date though. Her little skank ass was watching the truck too.

I started thinking about the times me and her had. She was a bad bitch, for real. Shawty looked foreign but she was white and black. Short, petite, tatted up, with long black hair and a bad attitude. That bitch belonged in a magazine, but she was too busy being stuck on hood shit. She ain't have no job so she was selling crack to be able to eat. I gave that bitch game, and she ran with it. It was what it was. I wasn't sweating no bitch or about to lose no sleep over one either. Finally, I decided to jump out after having waiting five minutes. Once they all saw me, their faces were priceless. Hating ass muthafuckas! I had just shat on they ass again and it was funny to me. My brother was the first one to say something and of course it was some bullshit.

"Boy, who truck you stole?" he asked me as I walked towards them.

His black ass was dressed in all black too, standing there looking like Wesley Snipes.

"I ain't stole shit, lil nigga stop hating! Fuck y'all niggas got going on round here?" I shot in response.

I reached my pocket for a cigarette, and I lit it as I looked at them niggas.

"Shit."

"None."

"Just coolin!" they all answered as I continued to smoke my Newport.

The sun had just dropped, and it was right on time because the hood was about to pop.

"Word?" I asked as I looked at the three.

Shay walked by right after that and made eye contact with me as she went into the store. I waited until I finished my cigarette and then I followed her inside. That little bitch was looking right so I wanted to see it again up close. I can't even front like I ain't miss that pussy. She was one of them shy freaks that like to suck dick with her head under the covers. She acted like that changed something though. Bitch I still know it's you! When I made it inside, I saw that she was at the counter buying a pack of Game cigarillos. She had on a pair of black leggings, a black tank top, and some black and grey Nike Air Max, which let me know that I had trained her right.

"What you looking at?" I heard her say breaking my concentration.

I had gotten lost in that ass just that fast.

"All that ass!" I said not bothering to try and hide the fact that I was behind her lusting.

That bitch knew what time it was with me, so I don't know why she was acting.

"Whatever, where Shannon at?" She teased bringing up my girl's name.

"I don't know, I ain't no babysitter!" I shot back as Ali gave her the change from her purchase.

"Whatever! What's up?" She asked me as she turned to face me with her cigarillos in her hand.

She looked me up and down checking my shit out. I knew my jewelry was like that but I wasn't really dressed up like I had been earlier. Even in all black though, everything I had on was designer.

"I'm tryna see now, but you wanna play, though!" I told her as I pulled her to me.

I had both of her ass cheeks in my hand as I squeezed them shits. That ass was stupid soft, and my shit was trying to stand up.

"Man, here you go!" She said stepping back and looking towards the door to make sure splash wasn't watching.

I didn't give a fuck though because I knew that nigga was pussy. He had been exposed his hand when I had got out. I wasn't beefing over no bitch though, so I let they ass rock.

"I'm for real! What's up with it?" I asked her knowing he knew what I was talking about.

She knew that I was trying to fuck. It wasn't really no secret.

"Boy, I'm not doing this with you! Get your life!" She said smiling before she walked out.

I couldn't do shit but laugh. Fuck that bitch! Walking back outside, I saw that two more cars had pulled up. I knew one belonged to my cousin Twan and the other one belonged to this bitch named Lil Lisa. Lil Lisa wasn't nothing but a jump off looking for a quick come up. She had been all in my inbox for the longest, but we never seemed to cross paths until now.

"Damn I gotta pull up in the hood to get at you huh?" I heard a female voice say.

Once I looked in the direction where it had come from, I saw that it was Lil Lisa leaning out the window of her car. She was pushing one of them little Buick Lacrosse shits that had just dropped but I knew it wasn't hers because it had a rental sticker in the window.

"I guess so. What's up with it, though?" I asked her ass I walked up to her window.

Lil Lisa was a dark skinned joint that kept micros in. She ain't really have no body because she was one of them skinny bitches. This bitch was a golddigger, so I wasn't really on it like talking about. I knew that bitch was after my sack, but I ain't have nothing for her.

"Shit! Tryna find some gas. Roll that shit up and smoke something with a bitch!" She said giving me that look like I was one of them sucker ass nigga's she was used to finessing.

I ain't gonna lie though, the shit worked like a muthafucka and at the same time I wanted that bitch shay to see that a nigga really wasn't pressed about no ho.

"Nah, you roll it up!" I told her as I went in my pocket and pulled that gas out.

I already knew the bitch was devious so I ain't give her my sack. Instead, I snatched two decent sized buds out and handed them to her.

"Damn, this shit looks like some fire!" She replied.

"Yeah, it is and don't pull off with my shit neither!" I said smirking even though I was dead serious.

"Boy bye, don't try to play me like I'm a broke bitch or something because we is eating!" She flexed as she flashed a nice little stack.

It wasn't nothing but a bunch of tens but it was thick though, so I guessed it was like two or three stacks.

"Man, put that little shit up before you get robbed!" I joked as I stepped over to the truck so I could get my phone.

Mils and JC were now outside as well and one of them had turned on the radio on full blast. I wasn't tripping though because I was gonna do the same thing. this was typical hood shit that I did on a daily basis.

"Who that right there?" Mils asked me as I read a text message on my phone from Shannon.

She wasn't talking about shit though so I ain't even respond before I slipped it into my pocket.

"Lil Lisa thot ass!" I told him as my cousin Twan started backing out.

That nigga ain't even never got out or if he did it was when I was inside the store. Nigga must've pulled up just to bust a play or something. I ain't really know and didn't really care but I watched as he slid off in his Sponge Bob Cutlass on eight's. That nigga was eating off that tree

"Oh yeah? Ask that bitch where her friends at?"

"Aight, but look go spin the block one time and see if you can get the rest of that off." I told him knowing damn well lil Lisa and her friends were out of his league.

All them little bitches was after that bag and he ain't have one so he was dead. And just like I thought he forgot all about the friend shit and ran and jumped in the Benz. JC went with him and I slid in the passenger seat next to Lil Lisa.

"So, when gonna stop playing and fuck with a real both, though?" She asked me as soon as the blunt was lit.

She had all the windows in and Lil Baby was coming through the speakers at a reasonable volume. I could see Rontay, Tez, and Splash as they passed a bottle of Cîroc around in front of the store.

"I ain't playing I just ain't with the fuck shit!" I told her once I had grabbed the blunt from her.

She was turned in her seat with her legs up under her facing me.

"What fuck shit?" She asked as if she didn't already know, and I had to give her that bitch please look.

That's when I noticed that she was wearing all white with a pair of all white Yezzy tennis shoes. The bitch was fresh as fuck but I knew she was looking for a sponsor though.

"See, that's the problem you think somebody after that little bit of money you making! Boy it ain't even like that, for real! I really be tryna fuck with you like for real!" She said with the serious face.

"You already know I got a wifey though!" I told her knowing she probably ain't give a fuck.

"I don't give a fuck!" She flexed confirming what I already knew.

Still, I wasn't convinced that it wasn't about the check because I knew how she got down.

"I bet you don't! Been what happened to you and that nigga you had a little while ago?" I asked her because I wanted to know.

Word on the streets was that she had got that nigga set up to get robbed.

"I know you heard what happened, so why even ask?" She shot back as if it wasn't nothing.

This bitch wasn't shit, but I had to respect the fact that she kept it all the way real.

"It ain't even how muthafuckas tryna make it seem. They on the outside looking in for real and don't even know shit! That nigga was some bullshit and he got what he had coming!" She flexed before taking a deep pull from the blunt that was now halfway gone.

"If you say so!" I said not really caring either way.

I wasn't worried about it because I never was the type to slip. I stayed with the pole and I knew for a fact that I would never let this ho get close enough to know my business.

"Anyway, what's up? You gonna let me taste some of this or what?" She questioned while at the same time reaching across the car to grab my dick through my jeans.

I'm what you call a horndog, so my shit responded out the gate. Next thing I knew she had my shit out my pants playing with it. I could tell she liked what she saw because she was making sounds that were turning me on. This bitch was a fool for real because it wasn't even no tint on the car so if a muthafucka wanted to be nosey all they had to do was walk up and look. I ain't care though because this bitch was jacking my shit like a fucking professional.

"You like that shit, huh?" She asked me in the freakiest voice she could muster.

I ain't say shit though. I just kept on watching her work as she watched me. Then she looked around, and right after that she leaned over the armrest and started sucking my shit. That bitch knew what she was doing to because she had my toes curling up inside my Jordans. I looked out the window over where I knew Shay was sitting and that bitch was staring like a muthafucka. She had her face frowned up like she was disgusted but I knew that the bitch was just hating.

Then I made eye contact with my brother right before he told Tez, and Splash to peep what I had going on. Now all the attention was on me and this how Lisa as she kept doing what she was doing. Five minutes into it, she started bobbing her head fast as fuck and I felt myself about to bust so I palmed her head and started fucking her face. It wasn't even thirty seconds later, and I was filling her mouth.

"Argh shit! You better not spit either!" I blurted out as I came in her mouth.

And just like that little ho swallowed that shit and then looked up at me with a smile.

Chapter Nine - Yella

Back on traffic, I was on my way to Budget Inn to meet Ginger and Muffin. It wasn't none but a three minute drive but the three stop lights I got caught and made it five. The Budget wasn't none like the Red Roof, Econo Lodge, Marriot, or none of that shit. It was like the trap away from the trap. A room ran like forty five dollars, but you could make like forty five thousand real easy. Anything went and all was for sale including crack, powder, dope, weed, and especially pussy! The only problem was with the Budget was that the muthafucka was hot as a firecracker. You could get jammed up real quick if you ain't know what you're doing. And even if you did you could still end up calling home collect.

That's why when I pulled up, I had to peep the scene because I wasn't trying to be doing no high speed chase tonight. I had to work, and a gun and I knew Mils had a strap as well. We was going straight to the fed's without passing go for real. When Ginger called, she told me that they were in room two twenty one. I already knew that the room was in the middle so I hurried up and pulled around so I could park and hop out. The Budget was shaped like a horseshoe, but you could drive in a circle because the parking lot wrapped all the way around the building.

"Ey yo, keep your eye open for then boys!" I said as I grabbed my phone and slid outta the truck.

Even have to knock because they already had the door open for me. Once I got inside, I saw that they had a trick and some more muthafuckas in there with them. It was cloudy as shit, and I could smell the stinking ass scent of burned crack in the air. It didn't bother me though because I was used to it.

"I'm glad your ass ain't take forever this time!" Peaches said from the corner where she was sitting.

Peaches was another one of my fiends that I served on a daily basis. I was surprised to see her at the Budget those GH because she had her own crib on Lathrop Street. It wasn't my business to ask, and I was trying to be in and out so I could get the fuck on.

"Yeah, yeah, what's up, though?" I asked as I looked around at everybody to see what the deal was.

"Let me get a gram, Yella! And I tryna hear all that other shit and I got my scale too bitch!" Muffin told me with a smile as she went inside her wig to get her money.

That bitch kept everything in her wig, and everybody knew it. That bitch had even saved me one time when the Heat Team pulled me over. She just so happened to be with me, and I had a little baby nine on me. tat bitch threw the strap in her wig and saved the fucking day. I ain't have no choice but to bless her with a big ass piece of crack after that. That bitch was my nigga when she wasn't fucking up.

"How much you got?" I asked as I whipped out my sack.

"Eighty!" She said as she handed me the money and the scale. It was one of them ten dollar joints you buy in the hood from the tobacco stores and shit.

"Aight, come on, man!" I said as I pushed the money in my pocket and then dropped the scale on top of the wooden dresser in the room. I was so good at eyeballing that the piece I broke off for her weighed one point one. I wasn't tripping thought because at the end of the day she was a part of the team. One by one I served Ginger, Peaches, and the other three before I peeled. I had gotten a call from another muthafucka while I was in there so that's where I was headed. It was looking like it was gonna be a good night because my phone and the block were both jumping. That's why before I went to my next trap, I dropped Mils and JC off at Fran's spot so they could catch anything that came through Briggs. Plus, I was trying to scoop up that little how Keisha because I wanted to continue where we left off earlier. Shannon had a radar on my dick though so before I could even hit old girl up she was on my line.

"Yo, what's up?" I asked her, answering the phone.

It wasn't like I could've sent her to voicemail because she was type to keep calling and texting until she got an answer. Then too, I ain't need her popping up in the hood trying to find me because that bitch knew how to get retarded. I wasn't trying to be on no domestic violence shit with her if I could help it.

"Come get me, I'm hungry!" She demanded and I could tell from her voice that she had a little attitude.

"Fuck wrong with you? Why you sound like that?" I asked her as I jumped on the highway.

I wasn't tripping because my play was right by the hotel so I could scoop her up on my way back.

"Sound like what? I don't sound like none, I'm good!" She assured me.

"Aight, be downstairs when I pull up."

"Where you at?"

"I'm about to go serve Jim and then I'm gonna be to get you after that!" I informed her.

She already knew who Jim was and where he stayed at so I ain't have to say nothing else.

"Aight!"

"Aight!" I shot back and then hung up.

I was like ten minutes away from Jim's crib. Jim was an older white dude I dealt with that lived in the Royal Oaks behind Chucky Cheese's. He had a blue Chrysler Aspen truck that I rented from time to time when I needed some wheels. I had been on some more shit lately though, so he was actually about to spend some money with me. At least that's what I was assuming until I pulled up and he jumped in the truck with a black duffle bag. That cracker was smiling like he had hit the lottery or something.

"Fuck is you smiling for, Jim?" I asked as I looked around paranoid.

He was growing me off for real and I ain't like that shit. What he said next made me calm down and smile all at the same time.

"Because I got something for you!" He claimed still smiling like something was tickling him to death.

"Fuck you got for me, Jim? I hope this is some money you done made me drive all the way the fuck out here?" I questioned with a raised eyebrow.

I was about to be all types of mad if this cracker had me on a dummy mission.

"Oh, I got something nice and it's better than money my boy!" He told me still smiling except now he was nodding his head with it.

His eyes were big as shit too and he was looking like the Joker from Batman on some other shit.

"Man, what the fuck you got, man? I ain't got time for no bullshit, yo!" I flexed because I was starting to get mad and I guess he knew it because the smile, on his face vanished real fast. Instead of answering though, passed me the bag and I looked inside of the bag.

"What you want for all this shit, Jim? I got seven grams for you right now! What's up?" I asked and made him an offering the same sentence.

That fool had a mini AR-15, a level 3 vest, and two 45's both of them chrome with pearl handles. I ain't give a fuck how or where he got them from. All I wanted to know was how I could get them.

"Seven grams?" He asked me as if he couldn't believe me.

The face he was making when he said it though made me laugh.

"Come on, man, you gotta do something better than that!" He added and I couldn't even be mad at him because the shit was in the bag was worth way more.

"What you tryna get?" I asked him again because I wasn't about to hang myself by offering more than what he was looking for.

Shit, I was a finesser, so I ain't getting finessed. "Mmmmm man, since it's you I guess you can give me the seven grams and a hundred and fifty dollars!"

"Jim, I ain't coming off no cash but I can give you ten grams though!" I said knowing he was gonna bite.

"Deal!"

"Aight, bet!" I said as I handed him a seven that I already had sitting to the side for something else.

It wasn't like he had no scale or nothing, so I knew he'd never know. After he looked at the bag and examined it for a minute, he nodded his head and then jumped out. After I threw the bag on the passenger seat I backed out and slid. The hotel wasn't none but like two minutes away, so I was there in no time. As soon as I pulled up, I threw the truck in park and hopped out with the bag. Wasn't no way I was about to be riding around with all that shit. Shannon wasn't even downstairs like I told her to be, so I had to group and grab her dumb ass. I wasn't tripping though because I had to get some more work anyway.

"Damn, bae, I ain't even know you was outside!" She explained as soon as I came through the door but I ain't responding.

For one, I swear I had told her to be outside and two I knew I have a smartass mouth, so I ain't want to say none to start no argument. Shannon had a little bit of mouth on her too and it wasn't no telling what might come out of it.

I threw the bag in the closet and then snatched up my Gucci bag to take with me. Once I had that I went over to the cereal box I had my money stashed and got it. I was down to my last three zips plus whatever I had left in the truck. I didn't plan on coming back to the room until after I had run out and then went and seen my plug. Shannon was gonna be stuck with me until the sun came up. I needed her anyway though just in case it got hot so she could drive.

Chapter Ten

As usual, Peewee and Forest were up to no good. They were scheming and plotting like always did as they sat across the street from the spot. Mils had hem watching the strip and they both had walkie talkies so they could communicate with each other. The radios were one of Yella's ideas and it proved to be helpful in more way than one. Which is why as soon as Peewee saw the two black and white Chargers bend the corner off Lathrop onto Briggs, he quickly put the radio to his mouth to inform Mils and JC what was up.

Sure as shit, the two police cars came to a stop directly in front of Fran's spot. They weren't there to run up in the crib though. They were just there to break up the crowd that was hanging around on the strip. They didn't have to say anything though, because everybody started breaking up into two's and three's going different directions like they always did when the police came through on their bullshit.

"Fuck ass police always hating brah, for real" Forest expressed out loud as him and Peewee made a left off Briggs on Holloway.

"Fasho!" Peewee agreed as they continued up Holloway past the Big Apple. Shadai, CeeCee, and Boosie's were a few feet in front of them and Porsha and another smoker named Hotdog was in front of them. Hotdog was a light skinned older muthafucka with a big bold head. He specialized in making his white girlfriend's trick for him so they could get high with the money they made.

"Man, one of y'all bitches give me and Peewee a hit so we can get out the street!" Forest said to anyone that would listen.

"Who you calling a bitch?" Shadai asked turning around. she wasn't offended though, because that how they talked to each other.

"Man, fuck all that! Put something on my stem!" Peewee demanded almost begging with puppy dog face as everybody kept walking until they reached the next corner where they all made another left onto Guthrie Avenue. No sooner than they made the turn, Mils came over the radio letter them know that the police had just pulled off. A couple seconds after that everybody watched the black and white shooting up Holloway. The way that they were speeding it was more likely that they had gotten a call. Whatever it was, everybody was happy to see them go.

"Here y'all!" Shadai offered handing a nice sized piece of crack to Peewee. Her and CeeCee had both put in a little bit apiece to share with their two block buddies. It wasn't no way that they could turn them down because the two had done the exact same thing for them at one point or another.

"See, that's why I love y'all bitches!" Forest admitted excitedly as he loaded his stem and then took a blast.

"Yep, yep and all the little kids went to school!" Peewee said while smacking his lips. He had a chest full of smoke that he didn't let go until he had to. As soon as he blew the smoke out that's when the high hit him full force.

"Boy, somebody need to kick Yella ass for having work this goddamn good I swear to God!" He added before he burst out laughing.

"Boy, you dumb as hell!" Porsha told him laughing even thought she was in compete agreement with what he said. No sooner than the words left her mouth, they saw a black car creeping down coming from Pack Ave. They had all just reached the corner of Guthrie and Lathrop when the car stopped at the stop sign. It sat there for a few seconds before it continued straight across and then pulled alongside them and the window dropped.

"What's poppin?" Ruga asked sticking his head out the window. Ruga was a young nigga who favored NBA YoungBoy. Standing Up straight he was near six four. He was one of them muthafuckas that was out to make a name for himself doing dumb shit instead of trying to run that bag up.

"What up!" Everybody replied almost at the same time. They all knew that he was up to no good most of the time and they were all wondering if now was one of those moment.

"Where that nigga Yella at?" He asked with a smirk on his face. From where they stood, they could see that Joog was leaned back in the passenger seat. It was nighttime, it wasn't a question if the two were riding with fire of not.

"Nigga, you know damn well ain't nobody about to tell you nothing! Especially not nothing about my nephew!" Peewee spoke up as Porsha handed him a short off of the cigarette that she had just been smoking.

"Save me some, brah" Forest told him.

"Damn, Peewee it's like that big brah? " Ruga asked as if he ain't already know the answer. He knew that wasn't none of them about to go against the grain when it came to Yella. For one, the nigga was crazy and two he was too good to them for them to even thing about turning on him. Not for a nigga like Ruga, who was grimy as they came.

"Straight like that!" he sang laughing but he was dead ass serious.

"That's crazy! Y'all muthafuckas spend something with a nigga I got that fire caine now!" he asked trying to advertise his product. Everybody already knew that his work probable came from Murk and that shit that Murk had was pure garbage. Even if it wasn't they was already good because they knew that Mils and JC had that for sure fire right around the corner.

"Man, don't nobody want none of that doodoo you got! Ginger already told us she got some straight bake from you that ain't even melt down! Gone back down to Hype Park with that bullshit nigga!" Forest said clowning like he always did. He wasn't speaking nothing but the truth though. Them Nigga was trying to bring back a brink off a baby and that was impossible.

"You know that shit some trash you can't even give that shit away, but you want us buy it!" Porsha said joining Forest with the jokes causing everybody to start laughing except Ruga and Joog.

"Aight! I should air this shit out!" Ruga threatened as he flashed his gun. He had a forty with a dick in it and a red beam that lit up every time he touched the trigger.

"Now you wanna shoot us cuz you got some bullshit!" Hotdog said shaking his head at the little nigga.

"Nah, I ain't gonna shoot! But tell that little nigga Yella when you see him that I said he need to holla at me before it be some shit!" He threatened before he pulled off bumping money man's song called how it feel.

"It ain't gonna be no one stop capping!" Peewee hollered after him knowing that Yella wouldn't even be the least bit worried. "That lil nigga gonna fuck around and make my nephew smoke his lil dumb ass!" He added as they all started walking again.

Chapter Eleven - JC

"Ey brah, I'm about to go in here and take a shit, you good?" I asked Mils as I got up. Shit had slowed down a little bit even since the police had parked outside. I knew that muthafuckas was still around though because even when it was hot the hood still jumped.

"Fuck you telling me for?" Mils asked not even bothering to look my way as he continued to play Call of Duty on the PS4 that Yella had set up in Fran's crib. Even though this was the spot, Yella still had a flat screen and a game in that bitch. He wasn't worried about nobody taking nothing because somebody was always there.

"Aight, lil nigga!" I shot back aggressively as I slid to the back where the bathroom was. I had to shit badder than a muthafucka but I also needed to do something else. That's why soon as I got in there, I locked the door and then sat on the toilet. Reaching in my pocket, I pulled out the bag of crack that Yella had left me with. He gave me and Mils a fourteen apiece to sell while he was out busting moves. Opening the bag, I broke off like a point two before closing it back and putting it up. That's right, I smoke. But I smoked on the low and don't nobody know. Once I took my blast it was easy for me to shit. Once I was finished with that, I wiped my ass and then got up. I was feeling good, but I was about to be feeling even better once I put fire to the blunt that I had behind my ear. I had rolled it right before I went to shit. Lighting it up, I inhaled and then blew the smoke out. I did that five more times before I left the bathroom so that it would cover the smell up. I ain't really want nobody knowing that I smoked so I tried to keep it hidden as best as I could.

Once I got back into the living room, I noticed that the house was now packed and my seat was taken. Peewee, Forest, CeeCee, Shadai, Porsha, Boosie, and Hotdog were all in the spot now and Peewee was the one in my seat. I already knew I wasn't gonna be able to get him to move so I didn't even try. Instead, I just passed the blunt to Mils, then went outside.

"Fuck it! I'll just post up out here!" I said to myself as I sat down in the chair that was on the side of the house. See, I ain't just start smoking because I thought it was cool or no shit like that. I Graduated from snorting to smoking by accident. Yeah, I know it sounds crazy but just let me finish and tell you how it all happened. See my baby mama Taylor be out there on the same block doing what all the other bitches be doing. I admit I turned her out to that ho shit, but I didn't know that the bitch was gone start smoking crack and all that shit, for real! If Yella knew I was smoking he would probably blank on me and call me all types of dumbasses, and a whole lot more I slip up and muthafuckas catch me. Muthafuckas like this nigga right here.

"Break bread, nigga" Peewee demanded with that stupid ass gin on his face. I really couldn't stand that muthafucka but I know if it came down to it he was gonna definitely tell Yella.

"I ain't got shit, brah. Mils got everything." I tried to lie because I had been smoking real heavy so really everything left was for Yella. Plus, I broke Taylor's dumbass off with something to get her started for the night. when Yella had dropped us off that bitch had been in the spot on the couch sleep. Me being me, I woke her ass up my smacking my dick on her lips a couple times until she opened her eyes. I ain't have to tell her what to do because I had a bitch trained.

"Nigga, stop capping! Yella already told me what he gave y'all and Mils, just told me he almost out but you not!" That nigga told me calling my bluff like a muthafucka.

"Man, goddamn, Peewee, you doing too much!" I flexed as I broke his ass off a dime piece so he would gone and get the fuck out my face. He was really starting to rob me with this black mailing shit and it had me about ready to just let my habit be known. Fuck it!

"Nah, nigga, I ain't doing enough!" He shot back as he loaded his stem while walking down the driveway towards Forest and who was waiting for him in the middle of the street.

"The fuck!" I said as I jumped up before I realized what was going on, I had felt something moving in my pocket, but it was just my phone vibrating.

"I'm tripping like a muthafucka, yo". I admitted to myself laughing as I peeped a text from Taylor asking me if I was still at the spot. I quickly responded yes and a minute later she sent a simple response that said OTW!

"Bitch better have some money I know that shit!" I mumbled as I put my phone back in my pocket after I saw that it was going on one thirty. Another thirty minutes or so, the block was about to jump like it did every night.

Chapter Twelve - Yella

M e and bae had been busting rounds all night long. I gave her ass one of them transformer Ex pills t keep up with me. He didn't smoke weed but me, I had been facing blunts all night. I had a bottle of Avion and we were damn near halfway through it. To say that we were lit was an understatement. Pulling up at the BP on the corner of hollow street and Alston Avenue, I saw that the parking lot was jumping. it was fiends everywhere and before I could even get back in, they were already running up to the truck trying to see who was inside it. I ain't make them wait long though because I had to hurry up and run in the store to buy something to drink before I fucked around and threw up. See, when you on them pills, you gotta stay with something to drink, because, once your mouth dry, you gone.

"Oh, Yella hold up, I was just about to hit you up!" One fiend said to me, but I wasn't trying to hear nothing until I had downed a whole orange juice. Sliding in the store, I went straight to the back so I could grab me three Tropicana orange juices. One of them I drank out the gate as I made my way back to the counter. Once I got there, the Arab behind the counter smiled at me.

"What's up, baby boy?" I asked him through gritted teeth trying my best to smile back. He must've known I was on one because he nodded knowingly. " Yo, let me get this, a pack of cigarillos and two pack of Newport shorts in the box.

"Aight, but look you know it's been crazy out here tonight!" he told me giving me the scoop like always did.

"Crazy like what?" I asked as I handed him a twenty for my shit.

"I mean, like, they everywhere, yo! I tell them leave and they leave and come back more muthafuckas! It's crazy, man." He explained shaking his head with a slight smirk on his face. That muthafucka favored Bruno Mars and he really thought he was black.

"You know how that shit be though, my nigga. This the hood, and plus all they traffic be really bringing you business, so you gotta take what else come with it!" I told him before I slid back outside where a small crowd of fiends stood waiting for me by the door. Jumping back in the truck, I served them out the window and then I slid off busting a left up Holloway. Two minutes later, I was pulling up on Briggs outside the spot where I saw Taylor jumping out of an old beat up station wagon. JC was standing at the end of the driveway like he was Magic don wang of something and everybody else was standing around like it was a fucking clock party of something.

"Man, why the fuck y'all ain't in the cut or in the fucking house? Come on, man, y'all muthafuckas is tripping yo, for real!" I hollered I hopped out because I know they knew better. Fiends sometimes be like kids, and I felt like I was they daddy of something because I had to always regulate and keep them straight. I had parked across the streets from the spot like always did because the law could fuck with something being guilty by association.

I ain't have to say nothing twice and I was glad because I was on them thangs and more than likely a muthafucka would've got slapped. I didn't plan on staying to long because I had to run up the highway and meet Bandanna. He had a play for me for a couple of hundred, so I had to go get that. I had to pull up and hit Mils and JC off with some more work. I couldn't just leave without making sure I left caine on the block because if I did, I would be having to turn right back around again. Once I did that though, I ran right back out the house and made bae jump in the driver seat so I could kick back and relax for a minute. It had been a long night and I just wanted to roll me a fat ass blunt and listen to Money Baggz about the life that I was really living.

"Where we going, bae?" Shannon questioned as she adjusted her seat before lighting a Newport and looking at me.

"We going to meet Bando right quick!" I told her to let her know that she needed to be heading to Raleigh. Then I typed the address that he had texted me into the built in GPS that came with the truck. After that, I turned the music up and then leaned my seat back. By the time we hit the highway I had my blunt rolled up with the window cracked to suck the smoke out.

Usually when I drove to Raleigh, it only took me like twenty five minutes, but since I had Shannon driving it took us damn near forty. I wasn't tripping though because ain't neither one of us have no license and I was dirty as fuck anyway so be so anyway so better safe than sorry. Once I heard the GPS answer that we were less than two minutes away from our destination, I harried up and hit Bands to let him know we were about t pull up. Looking at the clock on the dash, I saw that it was pushing up on three in the morning. I knew for a fact that my plug didn't pop out until like eight so that gave me five more hours to get my shit right. I was down to my last two zips not counting what I had just left in the hood because I knew that would be gone too.

Once we pulled up where Bandanna told me to come to, I saw him and two other muthafuckas that I had never seen before Waiting on us by the curb where his rental was parked at. I wasn't tripping though because I trusted my man with my life. Like I said this nigga was my nigga and he was a whole one hundred. Jumping in the backseat, he made the introduction and then went crazy like I knew he would!

"Boy, where the fuck you get this muthafucka? Look at this bitch with all this peanut butter wrapped around this muthafucka!" He flexed as he looked around giving it a nod of approval. He could see the interior clearly because I had the light on so I could see who he had with him. I trusted my nigga no doubt, but being in the streets still taught me to be paranoid and cautious of everything.

"You know how I do, brah! One of my fiends finessed this bitch and now I got it in the chokehold." I told him knowing He already knew the deal.

"What up with it, though, my nigga?" I asked him so we could handle business real quick. I wasn't trying to be rude I was just on a time schedule and a mission.

"Damn, nigga, you in a rush? You already dipped on me earlier!" He shot back chocking before he spoke to bay. I guess he had just noticed her because she hadn't said shit and had been leaning down looking at something shit on Facebook.

"What's up, sis, you don't know nobody now?" he asked her ignoring the look I was giving him.

"Nah, I was just looking at this fight! Some bitches was going at it in MacDougal earlier. What up, though?" She said looking back for the first time with a smile looking high was shit.

"Damn, y'all muthafuckas geeked up for real!" He said causing me, him, and bae to all laugh at his stupid ass. My nigga was a clown. Not a clown as in being lame but a funny as nigga though.

"Man, what up? Fuck, you had me slides all the way up here for?" I questioned still laughing at his ass. He was talking about we were geeked, but his ass was up at three right along with us. That nigga got his money from eight to five Monday through Friday. Then again, he was probably up swiping cards.

"Aight, what kinda deal you got for eight hundred? They had some jewelry too, but you know I went on ahead and snatched that, though!" he said as he passed me eight crispy ass blue face that themed through.

"They smoking?" I asked him as I dropped the money in the book bag that was open on the floor between my legs.

"Yeah, they smoking!" He told me.

"Look out for us, though, my man, and we'll be spending with you!" One of them said causing me to make eye contact with his Fred Sanford looking ass.

"Ey man, what I tell y'all before he go here? I'm gonna do the talking because he don't know y'all. He came way up here as a favor for me so chill out!" My nigga snapped with authority.

"It's cool, brah, I got something for them!" I assured going in my bag to get my scale. Unlike Muffin, I had a big boy that cost like fifty and some change. Once I placed it on the armrest, I folded up a dollar and dropped it on there to make sure It was weighing right. Once I did that, I put like nine grams on the scale and then I dumped it all into the plastic that I pulled off of my cigarette box.

"Here you go! fuck with me now. You can get my number from brah!' I told the Fred Sanford nigga as I handed him the work. "It gotta be worth it to make me come way up here though" I added once he had grabbed the work.

"What y'all fools about to get into?" Bandanna asked me after the two crackheads had jumped out leaving just us there in the whip

"Shit, nigga, you know how I do, I'm up!" I told him, and he shook his head because he already knew I was the going to sleep no time soon.

"Yeah, I already be knowing! I would ride with y'all but I gotta be around because it's the first tomorrow and you know I gotta push them checks out early!"

"I already know it. I'm tryna run through this little shit I got left so I can be ready by the time the sun come up." I told him trying to give him a hint to let me the fuck go, so I could finish doing what I was doing. I guess he got the message because after he dapped me up, he hopped out the truck and me and bae dipped. Checking what I had left, I guessed I was down to my last zip and a half or maybe a little bit more. After I did that, I counted all the money I had on me, and the total came up to twenty three bands. I was ready now because I had already told myself that I was gonna up the amount that I usually got.

So, instead of getting a nine, I was gonna go ahead and snatch up a half a brick. I ain't even have to fuck with the money I had stashed at my mama crib because eighteen zips wouldn't cost me nothing but fifteen stacks. I could get the whole thang for thirty, but I wasn't trying to rush it. I had come a long way by being patient and I wasn't trying to crash now.

Chapter Thirteen – Yella

By the time the sun came up, I had almost run through everything. Mils and JC were both out of work, so I snatched the little money they had and then gave them what I had left to split until I had hollered at my folk. Fran had been calling me nonstop telling me to bring her some work because muthafuckas out there needed it bad. I was being pulled in all type of directions and it made me smile because I loved that shit. I loved the hustle just like the fiends loved getting high. I was starting to get big in the game, but I just didn't notice how big until I hit my man's up! He ain't answer when I called him at seven or when I called back at seven fifteen. He did pick up though when I hit back a third time at 7:45.

"Yo?" he answered in a groggy voice so I could tell he had been asleep. Either that, or the nigga was faking. I didn't take him for a nigga that played games tough because was usually straight up with it and about his business.

"Ey what good, brah, you up?" I asked hoping he'd say yeah and come on out to meet me. I needed to get right asap because I still had to whip that shit before I would be ready to put it out there. I had a lot to do in a little bit of time because I was trying t beat everybody else that hustled to the punch.

"Yeah, what up what you tryna get, lil brah?" He asked me right before I heard him yawn.

"Shit, I need double what I usually get. I got the whole fifteen!" I told him to let him know I wasn't playing about it.

"Who this, Yella?"

"Yeah, nigga, this Yella! what up? You fuck with me or nah?" I asked because I was excited.

"Aight, meet me at the Bojangles!" he instructed me which is where we usually met up whenever we did business.

"You on the way now or nah?" I wanted to know because if he wasn't I ain't want to be just sitting.

"I'm putting yo shit together now!" he assured me before the line went dead.

"Bae, we need some gas in here." Shannon informed me as soon as I finished talking. We were sliding down Holloway also most past Juma's store and the BP was only two blocks away.

"Aight, cuz we need to switch places anyway so pull up at the BP." I instructed her as I reached on the floor to grab my strap. Even though the sun was up I was still on point. Especially being that we were so close to Hyde Park. I wasn't about to let them fuck niggas catch me slipping on some bullshit. Once we pulled in through, the parking lot was empathy except for an old lady with a Honda mini wan at one of the pumps.

All the traffic that had been there the night before was gone now. It was always like that though because of the simple fact that blue store and the Big Apple both closed at a certain time while the BP stayed open twenty four hours. Basically, the traffic bounced from one end of Holloway to the other depending on what time of day it was.

By the time I sent bae inside to pay for gas and she came back out, I filled the truck up. As soon as I was done, I hopped back in and slid out the parking lot and bent a lift at the light onto Alston

Avenue. It took fifteen minutes for me to get to the Bojangles off of Fayetteville Road. My mama's crib wasn't but another five minutes up the road, but I ain't have time to be fucking with dukes. I was on a paper chase trying to run that bag up. As usual when I pulled up, I didn't see my plug waiting so I hit his jack as I backed in by the trashcans and the drive thru.

"Yo, you there?" He asked as soon as he picked up.

"Yeah, you already know!" I told him as I started busting down a cigarillo. Since I had to wait, I figured I might as well roll up some wake and bake to get the day started. Really though my day had never ended because I had been up for three straight days grinding and I probably had another four or five in me.

"What you in?"

"I'm in a white Benz truck!" I told him as I noticed his truck turning in.

"I see you brah, I'm in the same spot I usually be at." I explained and then hung up because wasn't no need in still talking.

"Give it here, I'll roll it!" Bae told me reaching for the blunt so she could continue where I left off. I ain't say nothing because she was right on time. Instead, I grabbed the fifteen stacks that I had already counted twice and stuck it in my pants before I hopped out and hopped in with the plug, He wasn't one of them flashy niggas at all. He was pushing an old Chevy pickup that looked like something off of Jeepers Creepers.

"What up, baby boy?" He asked me as he gave me a pound while looking me in the eyes. He kinda put me in the mind of Suge Knight because they looked like they could be brothers.

"Same shit, my nigga!" I assured him as I handed him the cheese, I was ready to make the switch so I could got ghost.

"I gotta count this or it's all here? " He asked me with a smirk as he paused. He had been just about ready to throw it in the glove box when he did.

"Come on, man, now you're trying me! I ain't never been short so it ain't gone happen now, big dog!"

"Who truck you got? Crack rental hug? " He asked while he threw the money in the box and then reached under his seat.

"Yeah, you already know I like to switch it up." I told him as he pulled a small Spider-Man bookbag out and handed it to me.

"Yeah, I feel you. But check this out, you owe me fifteen, aight, that's a whole joint." He explained completely surprising me and catching me totally off guard because in all the times that I had ever dealt with the nigga he had never thrown me shit. NOTHING! Not even a fucking gram and now all of a sudden, he was pitching me a whole half a block.

"What you on?" I asked him to see what was because he was throwing me off right then for real."

"I ain't on shit, my nigga. I just see you working, and I been wanted to give you a push, but I had to see if you was really for real. I do straight business and I respect niggas who do the same. You been consistent and I see that so I'm trying to keep it that way." He said breaking it down to me. The nigga was weird as fuck, but I knew why he was the way he was though. Brah had done a dime to the door in the Feds because his own brother had set him up. Shit was fucked up, but it taught him how to be smarter. Real recognize real all day, so I guess he could smell it on me.

"Facts" was all I could say because in my head I was already plotting on what the fuck I was about to do. I had never held a whole brink in my life, I knew one thing though, and that was that I was about to turn shit up all the way.

"Aight, hit me when you ready, baby boy." He said smiling as he shot me a pound before I hopped out.

I ain't never did the speed limit in my life but I was doing it now though. It took me twenty minutes to get to 15-501 where our hotel was. Once I pulled up, I didn't park in a spot because I wanted Shannon to get us some breakfast. Just wanted to be in the room alone so that I could bust the block open and hide the half of it in the ceiling. I trusted my bitch but at the same time she didn't need to know everything until it was time for her to know. Yeah, true she had proven herself before but at the same time I knew that women moved on emotion, so you never really knew what a bitch would do or how a bitch would act in certain situation. the level of the game had changed so by law the way I moved had to follow. That eighteen was now twenty two and a half because I had managed to scrape an extra seven out of each zip.

By the time I finished all that, it was going one eleven o'clock and my phone was going stupid. I didn't even have time to wash my ass before I had to run right back out the door. Before I did that, though, I made sure to put up sixteen ounces and I took the rest and threw it in the Spider-Man bookbag that I had just gotten from the plug.

"What you gonna do? You staying or going cuz I'm about to slide? I asked as I looked at bae to see what she gonna say. Truth be told I needed her to ride because she was my second pair of eyes. I had her ass trained right so I didn't have to hold her hand in the field. I could drop her in the spot, and she would know how to run it without asking for directions.

"I'm not staying here, I know that!" She replied as she got up and grabbed her cigarettes and the keys to the Benz. Unlike me she had been able to shower and change clothes.

"Aight, let's get it, then!" I ordered as I cracked the door to peep out. Once I saw that the scene was clear I opened it all the way and we left. Our door always had the do not disturb sign out, so I never worried about leaving my shit in the room. Plus, if anything ever came up missing then everybody that worked at extended stay would as well.

Chapter Fourteen - Yella

Since Fran was the closest to where I was at, that was my first stop. The Carolina Duke was the same as the Budget. The only difference was that the two were on opposite sides of town and the Duke ran sixty five dollars a room. They way that the bitch jumped though made it worth it. As soon as I pulled up, I beeped the horn for Fran to come out. I was in a rush, so I wasn't trying to be there long.

"Hey baby!" Fran damn near yelled once she got in and saw that I had Shannon with me.

"Hey Fran!" Shannon spoke back plainly with a smile that I knew was fake. Fran was so high I thought that she couldn't tell the difference. Shannon really didn't like Fran because she felt like I be doing too much for her. I guess it was some emotional women shit she was on. You never could tell with Shannon because she was bipolar as fuck,

"Boy! I hope you brought something extra for that cracker cuz he tryna let you get the truck longer."

"Oh yeah? What he talking about?" I asked because that was exactly what I wanted to hear.

"Matter fact come on let's go holla at him" I added as I busted my door open while grabbing the Spider-Man bag from between bae's feet. Once we got inside, I negotiated with him and ended up getting the truck fr another week. His card was working now so the room he could pay for himself. On top of that, I left Fran with a whole zip to handle her business. I still had a few days left before I had to go to Enterprise and pay for the Challenger, so I wasn't worried about it.

Back on traffic, I made a couple stop here and there until I finally made it to the hood. As soon as I pulled up on Briggs, I saw Mils standing on the porch. As soon as he saw the truck, he ran over and jumped in. Once he passed me the chicken, he had me for, I reached in the bag and threw him a whole zip. I never gave that nigga that much work and he never had as much work either so his eyes got big when I handed it to him.

"Check this out, my nigga." I said as I turned around to look at him because I wanted him to see that I was serious.

"Keep shit rocking, how you been rocking and I'm gonna keep throwing it to you. Don't fuck my money up, Mils. I don't give a fuck what you do with yours as long as you make sure you got mine you dig?"

"Brah, I got you I'm ready now, for real!" he said with the serious face to get me to believe him. He had done the same thing a thousand times before though, so I wasn't convinced by the look. Really what had me was the fact that he had been holding shit down the right way lately.

"Aight, now cuz shit about to get real sweet so don't fuck around and get out cut off like you ain't paid the light bill." I told him. "Where that nigga JC at, though?" I asked him because the nigga had yet to show his face.

"Shit, yo guess is as good as mine cuz I ain't seen him since you left earlier!"

"Fuck, nigga probably chasing Taylor! Aight, I'm gonna hit line but let me slide though I gotta go make a play right quick." I told him before throwing the truck in drive as he hopped out. Once he closed the door, I pulled off and hit JC's phone. It went straight to voicemail, so I tried again and got the same results. His bitch was probably asleep somewhere. I wasn't tripping though. I would snatch that little paper up sooner or later. I ain't have time to be running him down because I had other moves to make. As soon as I bent the right on Lathrop, my phone went off and I peeped that it was my brother Rontay calling. Wasn't no telling what the fuck he wanted, and I was tempted to send his ass to voicemail, but something told me to answer. Luckily, I did though because he had some money for me.

"Yo?" I said picking up. I had my phone Bluetooth to the car so I could answer and call people by just pushing a button the on the steering wheel.

"Brah, you got some work? He asked back ass I bent a left on Park before busting a right on liberty street.

"I need a skon."

"How much you got?" I wanted to know as I bent a right on driver street and pulled up in front of TeeTee's house. TeeTee was a while, which I dealt with sometimes when I needed a quick place to cook up. I also used her spot to trap out of and to meet up with people who were trying to see me.

"A band."

"Gotta have eleven, brah!" I let it be known because that's what it was going for. Really a zip cost twelve and sometimes thirteen of fourteen if you run across a sucker. If it was a fiend, then the price went up to two flat.

"Goddamn, you gonna do me like that, lil brah?" He asked me which made me bay look at each other with that face like he can't be serious. I know the nigga was though because that's just how he give it up. He was always trying to get over on a muthafucka and it didn't matter who as long as it benefitted him.

"You want it or not? I ain't trying to sell no weight anyway to be honest!" I told his ass and I meant that shit because I knew my shit was some drop. If he wasn't trying to kick out what I wanted, then he could go and fuck with who he had been fucking with and get that garbage. Either way, I was gonna eat regardless.

"Yeah, man, where you at?"

"Pull up at TeeTee house!" I instructed and then hung up before he could respond. I ain't have time to be playing games with that nigga. Brother or not, business was business.

I tapped the horn twice to let Teetee know I was outside since she hadn't stepped out yet. I had been out there for like three minutes and she still hadn't come out. Once I beeped the horn though, she came out speed walking. She was built like a black chick and favored the white girl from the show the parkers. The onle difference was that she looked older because she was in her early forties.

"Wassup, Bully?" She asked me hopping into the backseat. She liked to call me Bully because she said that I looked like a Pitbull. It wasn't the first time I heard it, so it was all good.

"Same shit, different toilet!" I told her as I grabbed the two crispy blue faces that she was handing me.

"Yeah, well I owed you one twenty, so give me eight worth!"

"I got you, but look, though, I gotta proposition for you!" I said as I turned to look at her so I could see her face.

"And what's that?" She wanted to know looking me in the eye with a smile. Freaky ass white bitch. She had come on to me before, but I had turned her down because I ain't really do the white hos. She was thinking though but I wasn't on it like that.

"I need you to pump some work out your crib for me so I can lock this side of the hood down." I explained to her. Even though I had work two blocks over I still wanted some there because her street popped just like Briggs. In my hood almost every single street did its own numbers. that's why I liked to do Laps because it was always something or somebody looking.

"You didn't even have to ask that!" She assured me. "But what my cut and how much do I put aside for you?" she asked me causing Shannon to cut her eye at her. Bae didn't like TeeTee either because she thought that she was trying to fuck me.

"I'm gonna shoot you an ounce and I want fifteen hundred back. The rest is yours. You already know it three for twenty around here but if you can finesse to make you some extra then that's on you. I don't care as long as you have my cash right when I come to get it." I explained before I paused to make sure she heard me. When she nodded, I continued where I had left off at.

"Aight, now don't play no fucking games TeeTee because I ain't gonna be tryna hear no bullshit about you lost it or somebody stole it or none of that dumb shit you might try and come up with!" I said to make sure she understood exactly where I was coming from. I know she knew not to play with me though because I had smacked her up before behind my gun going missing one day.

Come to find out somebody really had stolen it but at the time I wasn't trying to hear shit.

"Come on, Bully, I got you! She assured me before I handed her a whole twenty eight. I was down to the last two that I had on me, and I was about to see another one go as soon as brah pulled up.

Chapter Fifteen – Bandanna

Thumbing through all them bands had my muthafucking hands hurting for real. Shit was crazy because the day wasn't even over yet. I always did big numbers on the first the third, and the fifteenth. So far, I had counted ninety thousand and I still had a little bit more to go though. I hadn't made all this cake today though, some of it was a part of my stash. I always checked behind myself and Krystal to make sure that she wasn't stealing from me. I didn't trust no bitch when it came to money because hos are greedy by nature. It took me another hour to run through the rest and the total came out to be ten bands short from two hundred grand.

Once I threw everything in the safe that I had in my closet, I slid out the door and jumped in my rental. Looking at my rolly, I peeped that it was going on three thirty. Another hour and a half and all the banks would be closed. I was waiting on Finesse to hit me up and let me know who shit went but until then I was gonna go and chill with my new little thang. It took me ten minutes to get to Raleigh North where little mama lived.

"Call Yas Jolly!" I ordered my iPhone and a couple second later I heard ringing coming through the car speakers.

"Hello?" A voice answered that I was starting to get familiar with. Me and old girl had been kicking it on the phone since we met, and this would be the second time we kicked it in two days.

"Yeah, I'm outside. You ready?" I asked her as I started busting down a vanilla Dutch. I didn't use cigarillos because all I rolled was three point fives.

"Yeah, I was already on my way out the door. I saw you pull up."

"Aight, say less." I said before pushing the end button on the steering wheel. By the time Yas got into the car I was just lighting the blunt. I had to do a double take because for some reason Shawty was looking extra good today. She was rocking a pair of yellow Levi's with a white and yellow POLO woman's button up top. She had a matching white and yellow Michael Kors' bag with a white, yellow, and royal blue Jordans. She had her hair flat-ironed, so it hung past her shoulders almost to the middle of her back and led down to a nice petite ass. Yas was mixed with black and Panamanian which is why she had coffee colored skin with blue eyes. She favored the singer Elle Mae and had an accent that sound lie she came from up top somewhere.

"Damn, you looking good as fuck, for real, Shawty!" I had to compliment that bitch because she was gorgeous.

"Thank you! I was just about to say the same about you." She shot back as she peeped me in True Religion from head to toe. I had Louboutin sneakers on my feet and my dreads were braided back in five neatly parted rows.

I knew I was looking good and the thick ass chain around my neck only added more sex appeal to my huge ego. I had gotten it custom made with a big four by five inch charm to match my four finger ring. I knew I had smoked they ass with this one and I couldn't wait to snap a picture so I could post it on my Facebook and tag Yella in it.

"I hear you! So, what's up? What you tryna do?" I asked her as I mashed out.

I hit the blunt two more times and then passed it to her.

"It don't matter, I ain't got nothing planned' she told me as she took the blunt from my hand.

"You don't be fuckin around in Durham or nah?" I wanted to know because that's where I planned on going. I wasn't trying to bump into Krystal or nobody that knew her. I was trying to chill with my man's since we hadn't really kicked it like we usually did.

"I been to that mall South Point, but I ain't never chilled in the city, though. Why you ask me that?" She wanted to know at me all crazy.

"Nah, it ain't none like that I was just asking because we about to slide down there!" I told her as I took the exit to jump on the highway. I had that new Money Bagz playing softly but once I saw that shit, ain't have no more questions I jacked it up to the max. By the time we made it to Durham I had make her roll up another blunt so I would have one ready to blow as soon as we pulled up on bra. I had already hollered at him, so I knew to meet him out 15-501 where his little room was at. I still couldn't understand bra sometimes because I knew he was getting all that money but still live out a hotel. Fuck it! I wasn't stunting it because it wasn't none of my business.

Pulling up, I looked around to see if i saw the truck that brah had been pushing but I didn't. I didn't see the Challenger either. I did see his Lexus that he barely drove though. It was purple with purple and chrome twenty two inch Gucci rims. I had been with bra when he copped the car way before it had rims, tint, or anything. Right beside it sat another car, this one was a two door box caprice that was also his. That shit was plain as hell though because he hadn't done shit with it yet except tinted it out. The tint was so dark that you couldn't even see in that muthafucka. Before I could even park, I saw brah bend the corner and slide into a handicap spot near the steps that led up to his room. Parking beside him, I cut the engine and grabbed my Gucci bag before me and Yas got out.

"You can hop in the truck, my nigga, I'm just running up to grab some more work." Brah told me as he and Shannon went up the steps.

"Wassup, sis?" I asked speaking to Shannon as they went up. She ain't say nothing but instead shot me a smile and wave. I already knew bra was dropping her off, so I hopped in the front seat and Yas got behind me. I heard that Lucci coming through the speakers, so my head automatically started nodding to the beat. It took Yella fifteen minutes to come back down, and I peeped that he had changed his clothes, so I knew why. I also noticed that he had a kid spider-man bag in his hand, and it made me laugh.

"Brah, what the fuck you doing with that?" I asked him still laughing as I looked at him once he got in.

"Oh, you got jokes nigga?" He replied as he backed out real fast.

"Nah, I'm just saying fuck is you doing with that cheap ass bag?" I asked him again causing Yas to laugh this time.

"Oh, so both y'all think it's funny?" Yella asked as he looked at me and then back at her before facing the road again. "Who you is anyway?" He asked looking at Yas in the rearview mirror.

"I'm Yas!" She answered before I could even introduce them.

"Yas, huh? Fuck you doing with this bum?"

"Aight! I ain't never been no bum! Clown!" I shot back in response to his little sneak diss. I knew he was just bullshitting, though. "Fuck is we about to get into though?" I wanted to know as I put fire to the blunt.

"Shit you already know how to do it! I'm about to go pick up my lil joint right quick first, though!"

"Who you talking about? " I asked him as we jumped on the highway.

"That lil thang you seen with me!"

"Oh, word?"

"Word!" be replied before he turned the music all the way up.

Chapter Sixteen - Keisha

I had been texting Yella all day. I don't know what it was, but I really wanted to see him bad as hell. I was feeling that nigga and I ain't even know him like that. Whoever said love at first sight didn't exist was lying because it was real. The last time I had seen him I was wearing jeans. This time I decided to throw on a skirt dress that stopped a couple inches up. You know you gotta let the pussy get a little air every now and then to keep it fresh. I backed off of the sneakers today and threw on my white Chanel sandals that were the same color as my dress, I knew I was looking good to because the picture I had posted on Facebook had a hundred like already and it had only been thirty minutes. I was looking like a whole snack, and I was praying that Yella was hungry.

I threw my kinky twist into a ponytail when I heard a horn blow. I knew it was Yella because wasn't nobody else around this way that ghetto. I wasn't tripping, though, I was just glad he didn't take forever. Once I grabbed my white Chanel bag off the bed, I was out the door. That's when I saw that Yella was in a white Benz truck. I remembered it being at the store the day before wen he had dismissed me to go handle his business. I had been a little salty though until my cousin had put me up on game.

"Damn, you looking something fire!" That boy that Yella had went and met said to me as he hopped out the front and left the door open for me to get in. That nigga was a fucking flirt for real, but he wasn't my type. Still though, I didn't want to be rude, so I thanked him.

"You're welcome!" He shot back before I jumped in the truck and smiled over at my future baby daddy. I shot back before I Jumped in the truck and smiled over at my future baby daddy. I didn't have any kids, but I was going to try and make one with his ass though.

"What's up? "Yella asked while trying to play me. Shit, I don't give a fuck if I was being worrisome or not. As long as his ass slid through, I was gonna do whatever worked.

"I am not!" I fired back playing dumb as he pulled off. I inhaled through my nose and the scent of new leather invaded my nostrils.

"Nah, you straight!" He assured me with a smile before he did the same shit he had done the first time he picked me up. I had to tell him about that music shit, but it could wait until another time.

As we rode, I found myself checking him out the same way I did before. He was looking fresh as fuck in a crisp red, white, and blue Armani button up with white True Religion jeans that had blue stitching. He had on a New England Patriots strap back that went with his shirt, pants, and the new Lebron's that had just dropped the past weekend. He had on his jewelry, and I could tell that he had added a peace or two to what had been hanging around his neck the first time I had seen him. He was looking like a rapper and his boy was too. I had noticed the little bitch in the backseat, but she hadn't spoken to me, so I didn't acknowledge her either. I wasn't there to make friends. I was trying to get fucked!

"You feel like rolling us up a blunt?" Yella asked me, turning the music down to hear my response. We were sitting at a light at the intersection of Holloway and Hyde Park.

"Yeah, I can! I ain't smoked all fucking day either!" I confessed as he passed me a sandwich bag full of gas and a pack of cigarettes. Turn the music back up while the light changed, Yella kept straight until he got to Park Avenue and bent a right. As soon as he made the turn he pulled over where three people was standing on the sidewalk. I didn't know them personally but did remember two of their faces from before.

"What good, Peewee?" I heard him ask as one of them after he turned the Radio down.

"We need fifty piece, nephew!" I heard the dude reply, which caused Yella to pull out a big bag of some shit that I assumed was work. A minute after that we were in motion again and bending a left down Lathrop where some more people was waiting. I had witnessed him make almost two hundred dollars in ten minutes as he did a complete circle around the block. I also noticed that he had a lot of that white shit inside a Spider-Man bookbag that rested beside my feet on the floor. I also peeped that his boy had a Gucci bookbag back there with him, but I had no clue what the inside of his held. I also saw that Yella was stuffing his money inside the armrest. I wasn't being nosy, I was just very observant of my surroundings. Being in the military had taught me to stay on point and on my toes.

That's mainly the reason why I went and got my gun permit and now carried my purse rocket everywhere I went. We bent a few more corners and ended up on the south side near Phoenix Square. I had peeped the street sign and it told me that we were on a little small side street called Dawkins. When I say it was crack heads everywhere like roaches, that exactly what I mean. They even had a fire going inside of a barrel beside an abandoned house that they were running in and out of. As soon as we pulled over a nasty looking bitch walked up to Yella's window calling herself trying to look sexy. Bitch please if she only knew! That's what I was thinking inside my head as I watched the exchange.

"What's up, Tamika? Where Buck at?" Yella asked her and I guess that when she realized it wasn't a trick inside the truck.

Smacking her teeth, she replied. "He over there stuck nodding off that dope! What's up want him?"

"Yeah, tell that nigga to hurry up. He had just called me a lil second ago so see if he still want that?" Yella explained causing that nasty bitch's eyes to light up.

"Oh, you the one he called? Shit, fuck him! He called for us!" She said before she looked over her shoulder and yelled, "Ey y'all the work right here!" which caused everybody to pause before heading in our direction.

"Nah, hold up, let me get out cuz I ain't try'na make the truck hot!" Yella said as he grabbed the bag that he had sitting in the cup holder. Once he jumped out, he led the crowd back over to where they had been before by the fire. All three of us watched as one by one, he took care of all of them. It took about ten minutes before he came back but what he threw in the armrest made it look like it was worth every single minute.

Chapter Seventeen - Yella

As soon as I left off Dawkins, I pulled straight up on Linwood and served CeeCee. I ain't even asked her what she was doing on that side of town because I already knew how she got down. That bitch was gonna be wherever the money was at. It was all good because I needed my clientele to move around, and I knew she would put the word out. Swerving off I bent back around the block doing a circle around Lincoln health Center before I spent a right back on Fayetteville.

Five minutes later, I was back in the hood and bending a right on Holloway. I don't know if I had bad luck or nah, but it always seemed like I got caught at the light where Hyde Park intersects. That's when I saw that ho ass nigga Ruga bending a right down Hyde Park. I knew it was his bitch ass because he had the window down and I knew what his car looked like. I started to send something as his ass but by the time I thought about it he was already sliding up the street. Once the light turned green, I slid through all the way up to Briggs and went a right. As soon as I did, I saw Mils flagging me down like he was on fire of something.

"What up?" I asked curiously seeing the murderous look he had on his face. Not to mention he had his strap in his hand and it was stuck on ugly so I knew something had just happened.

"Man, that bitch ass nigga Ruga just swung through and shot the spot up!" He told me which pissed me off instantly because I had just seen the fuck nigga.

"Ain't nobody get hit?" I asked as I looked towards the spot to see if I peep any casualties.

"Nah, stupid ass nigga ain't see me coming out the store so I upped the pole on him. He almost ran me the fuck over, but I kept shooting though. I shot that nigga driver side window out though." He explained to me down the smallest detail.

"Same nigga, huh?" Bandanna asked from the backseat where he had been listening the whole time.

"Yeah brah, nigga called it dead, but I see he back at it!" I told him but I was still looking towards the spot. That's when I saw that a little Honda was backed in the driveway." Who car is that?" I asked Mils as an idea popped in my head.

"JC driving that shit. He say he got it all night. But brah, what the fuck we gonna do about that nigga Ruga though?"

"Nigga, just chill I'm about to be right back and tell that boy JC don't fucking move until I get back!" I shot back before I sped off. A minute later I was pulling up on the driver street where my grandma's house was. She had passed away, but the house was paid for. Pulling up the driveway to the back, I parked and jumped out. I ran straight to the shed and reached up under it where I had my drako stashed. I ain't even have to check the drum because every gun that I owned stayed loaded and plus I was the only one that knew the gun was there. Jumping back in the truck, I turned it around in the backyard and drove back down the driveway. A minute later, I was pulling back up on the spot where JC, Mils, and Peewee were all waiting.

"Ey brah, jump in the driver seat right quick while I ride with them!" I said looking back at Bandanna.

"What nigga? You crazy as fuck if you think I ain't riding!" He fired back at me making me laugh.

"Say less!" I said nodding before I turned to the little bitch Keisha.

"Now I'm gonna trust you with my shit but don't try me like a lame though!" I said giving her that look that said I wasn't the one to try. I had close to seven bands or a little over inside the armrest, a four piece, and my FN. I was taking a big risk, but I wasn't worried because I knew where that bitch lived.

"Use something out the armrest and go to the liquor store right there in the village and get us something to drink! Whatever y'all get I don't care as long as it get us all that cheap shit." I instructed before I added " By the time y'all get back we should be back!" Just like I knew she nodded and then climbed in the driver seat once I hopped out.

"Ey yo, JC, you driving! Peewee hold the spot down for a minute!" I ordered with the Drake in my hand as I walked up to the passenger side of the little dusty Honda accord. That bitch looked like a ninety one, but I didn't five a fuck because it was the right kind of car for this mission. I Jumped in the front passenger seat with Bando behind me and Mils beside him. Me, Mils and Bando all had beams on out shit and all three of them were lit up like a Christmas tree. It wasn't no music playing or noting. The only sound that could be heard was me flicking my lighter to light my cigarette as I told that nigga JC where to drive to. I already knew that nigga Ruga had ran straight back to Hyde Park because i had just seen his ass at the light. Something told me to air his shit out then, but I didn't. It was all good though because I was about to let this little big bitch spit. The first time we spent the block we ain't see the nigga, though. I told JC to slide through Spruce Street a block over to see if I saw his ass out there. Bingo! I saw the car before I saw him, but I knew he was in it because it was moving.

"Yo, just follow that nigga until he stop!" I told JC as we slid down Spruce. I saw Ruga make a left on Gilbert Street, and we made the same left a few seconds later. That when I saw that he had pulled over in front of this fiend's crib that everybody in the hood called Ms. Kathy. JC was smart enough to pull over until he got out ant that when I looked back at bandanna to give him the play.

"Ey yo, check this out! I know that nigga Joog with him so do the nigga in the passenger seat and me and Mils got Ruga." I told him right before Ruga hopped out and JC hit the gas. As soon as we slid up on that nigga, I came out the window firing while Mils sat on the back window seal throwing shots over top of the car that we were in. As soon as the shots started ringing off that nigga Ruga hit the ground and didn't move or get back up. I didn't even have to check on Bando because I saw his workout of my peripheral.

"Go, go, go, go!" I yelled at JC who acted like he was stock or something. Me yelling in his ear brought him back though and we were moving a second later. A minute after, we were pulling up on Briggs where we all jumped out s if the car was on fire. In all actuality it was because we had just rode on some muthafuckas in it.

"Ey, JC gone ditch that car and get it the fuck away from here!" I said seriously because I knew if it got tied to the spot then it would lead to me eventually and I wasn't trying to go through it.

"Peewee do something with this car for me and Mils keep yo ass in the spot and don't came out. If you need something from the store or some shit like that then send JC or somebody!" I ordered before I looked at JC and then ran to go jump back in the truck that had just slid up. My blood was still pumping as me and Bandanna got back in, but I quickly vanished because Keisha passed me a lit blunt as soon as my ass hit the leather seat.

"You good, brah?" I asked bands as I hurried up and pulled off headed from my grandma's spot on driver. I had to get that gun away from me ASAP.

"Hell yeah, nigga, I do this shit!" He shot back laughing making me join him.

"Let me hit that blunt!" He demanded once out laughter had subsided. By then I was sliding up the driveway at my grandma's house.

"Let's switch!" I told him as I gave him the blunt and took his gun. Before he could even protest, I was already hopping out with it and the drako. Putting the Drake where I got it from and adding Bandana's, I then went over to the doghouse and reached inside where I had a couple pistols stashed. I grabbed the first one I put my hand on which happened to be a Glock forty with a stick. Once I had it in my hand I jumped back in the truck and gave it to my nigga.

"That's you, baby boy! I told him before I threw the truck in drive so I could turn in around.

"Shit, it better be after you done fucked mine up Nah, I'm bullshitting you already know!" he shot back as he examined the new toy I had just given him.

"Already!" I said before I looked over at Keisha. "So, what y'all get?" I wanted to know because I needed a sip bad as hell.

"We got some Cîroc!" She replied smiling and then added " Me and her was in there debating before we decided."

"Yeah, cuz I was like everybody drink Cîroc!" Yas added from the back laughing. By the way that they were so giggly I could tell that they had already cracked the bottle open. I wasn't tripping though because that's what I bought it for.

Chapter Eighteen - Ruga

As soon as the shots stopped and I heard the tires squeal, I rolled over so I could up the pol. I was a little too slow, because whoever it was had already bent the corner. I had a pretty good idea though. I was wondering why Joog ain't up and when I got to my feet I saw why. Every window on my car was shot out and Joog was in the front seat dead with his body full of holes. I ain't have time to be shedding no tears though, That nigga was already gone and I needed to be getting ghost next. Running to the car, I reached in and snatched his gun, put phone, and the little bit of weed I had in the cup holder. I didn't care about the car. It was mine but it wasn't in my name thought. I was just about to dip when I remembered to run his pockets. Shit, he wouldn't be needing it anyway so who better to have it than me?

Once I had everything, I dipped across the street and then jumped the fence so I could get to the next street over. I could hear the sirens already which let me know that somebody had called the law. I knew that was gonna happen because I don't know what the fuck them niggas were shooting but it sounded like a choppa and some more shit. As soon as I heard the first shot, I dropped and played dead. There wasn't shame in my game at all. Sometimes you gotta play position to avoid becoming a victim. I was only twenty which was way too young to dic in my cycs. I had way too much thuggin left in me to be getting smoked this early in the game.

It took me five minutes to get to the top of Spruce and then another three to get to Hyde Park where my bitch Narissa lived. She was really from Turnkey, but I had convinced her to get a spot in my hood. Throwing my key in the lock, I let myself in and locked the door back. That's when I finally took a long deep breath and thanked god for seeing me through another episode.

"Damn them fuck niggas killed my dog." I hollered in frustration before running to the room that me and Narissa shared. I went straight to the bed and lifted up the mattress where I kept my Sk. If them niggas wanted to play, then that's what we were going to do. Shit had been going on for too long anyway with all the back and forth. Now somebody had finally gotten touched, and it just so happen to be me. I still couldn't believe that them niggas just killed my muthafuckin nigga though. Shit was real before but it was for real now. I had to hit back but it couldn't be no more missing. It was time to spank something and leave it like they had left my dog.

That's when I got to thinking. I needed a way around since them nigga had fucked my shit up. I ain't have but a fourteen left and I was glad because I knew my shit was garbage. I couldn't even complain though because the nigga Murk was throwing us that shit. At the same time though it wasn't no point in having the shit if I couldn't move it. Scrolling through my contacts as I sat on the bed with the rifle in my lap, I stopped on the name Doc. I knew Doc would drive me around and wouldn't care about what I did out his car as long as he was smoking. I had something for them niggas. I was about to turn up for the streets.

Chapter Nineteen - Yella

The sun went down, and Gilbert Street was still taped off. Shit was crazy though because the word had gotten back that Ruga wasn't dead. I couldn't believe that shit though because I swear, I had hit that nigga. It was all good though I wasn't tripping because at least we had got one of them niggas. I knew that since Joog was always in the passenger seat he was more than likely the one that had been doing the shooting.

I sent Keisha and Yas to go check shit out because wasn't no way I was walking up to the scene and I knew my nigga wasn't either. They had just gotten back in the truck where I had parked and waited on Spruce. Now we were sliding up Holloway until I swerved and bent a left on Alston. I was about to hit the highway and take Bandanna back to his car so he could peel back to Raleigh. I made sure to drop him off in front of the hotel because I knew that my room was in the back and I ain't want Shannon to peep me outside. I didn't peel until I saw Bandanna pull back around though. Tapping the horn twice and flicking the light, I slid out and went left while he went right.

Now it was just me and Keisha in the Benz and I knew she was feeling saucy because we all had been knocking the bottle down and blowing blunts back to back. We were almost to her crib before she said anything. I guess she finally realized that I was taking her home and she wasn't ready to go yet.

"Where you going?" She asked me with her face twisted up as she looked at me like I was crazy.

"I was about to drop you off!" I told her straight up. Shit, I was trying to sit my ass down somewhere for real. It wasn't time to be running around right now. At least not until shit really hit the fan as far as what the police had or didn't have. I knew that we hadn't slipped and left no evidence, but I didn't know if anybody saw anything, or if Ruga was talking, or what. Even though I figured he would try and keep it on the street I still wanted to be safe.

"You coming in this time?" She asked me seductively as she eye fucked me while biting her lip causing my dick to stand up out the gate. I was kind of bent and I was on a pill, so it wasn't no question. I had to see what that little pussy was hitting for.

"Yeah, I'm definitely coming in!" I assured her as I bent a left into her neighborhood.

"Listen, turn this down. I stay around some Boogie was people they will complain to the office about this music." She told me after turning the music all the way down.

"Why you ain't been said none?"

"It's all good just remember from now on." She said and I just nodded as I parked in front of her crib. We didn't say anything else as we got out and I followed her in. Once we got in, I looked around as she led the way. Shawty had her shit laced, for real.

"You want something to drink?" She asked me as I sat down on the white leather couch that she had in the living room.

"Yeah, you got juice?"

"Apple? Orange? Pineapple?"

"Let me get some orange juice."

"Aight, hold up a second. You can turn on the TV if you want to. Make yourself at home." She offered before she went to the kitchen and got my drink. Once she brought it to me, she left and ran upstairs where I heard the water turn on a couple minutes later.

While she was gone, I looked around and surveyed my surroundings. Everything was white including the entertainment system that held the Sony flatscreen that she had. When I had took in everything, I gave it a nod of approval and then checked my phone. I had a text from bae, so I hurried up and texted her back to let her know that I would be home in a hour or two. Five minutes later I heard the water cut off. A few minutes after, Keisha came back down ass naked looking like a goddess! My mouth got watery just looking at that bitch as she walked over to me giving me that look like she wanted to eat a nigga up.

Without saying a word, that bitch dropped to her knees between my legs and undid my Ferragamo belt while looking me in the eyes, unzipped my pants and then pulled them all the way down to my ankles. My dick was already standing up and she hadn't even toughed that muthafucka yet.

I quickly found out that she was a head doctor though because she didn't waste time before she had her mouth wrapped around my dick. She started off by sucking on the tip and then licking it. next she went down to my sack where she sucked my nuts into her mouth one by one and then both at the same time. She wasn't giving me that nasty top with all that spit and I was glad because I ain't like that sloppy shit. She cleaned her mess up as she went making sure to suck her spit back into her mouth as she deep throated my length. she bobbed her head slow and then fast. This bitch was a pro and she had me cumming within minutes. She didn't stop. She swallowed that shit like a champ and kept going until my shit got back rock hard. I ain't even gonna lie after I had nutted and she kept sucking till I felt like I was about to pee in her face.

Once my shit got back right, she turned around and then lowered herself down onto my lap where she started riding me in reverse cowgirl. I was loving the sight because she was working that little phat ass and she knew that shit. She was looking back at me to see my facial expression and I was biting my lip as I gripped her ass checks and spread them so my dick would go inside her. I let her ride for a few more minutes before I flipped her ass over and threw her legs over my shoulder.

I had that ass bent up in the corner of the couch tearing that shit up. That pussy was stupid wet, and I could hear it farting and squishing as she moaned and begged for more. Once I felt her shaking up under me, I already knew she had just come so I switched position and picked her ass up in the air and fucked her while I stood in the middle of the living room.

"Oh my fucking God, I love you!" She screamed as she started shaking again. This time though that bitch squired and blew my mind because I had never witnessed a squirter until then. Switching positions again, I put her down and made her bend over the couch as I went back in and got right back to it. I did it all to that bitch. Smacking that ass, choking her, and I played with the clit while at the same time stocking it fast and deep.

"Argh shit! Fuck!" I said through gritted teeth as I fucked her.

"Yeah! Yes! Fuck me, bae! " She screamed back as she threw it back causing our skin to smack and sound off loudly.

"Who pussy this is?" I asked her as I felt my nuts tightening up which was a sign that I was about to nut.

"Yours, baby! It's yours!" She promised as them legs went to shaking again and that pussy got wetter.

"Ahh shit, I'm about to bust!" I admitted as I felt it coming through my pipe. It was feeling so good and intense that I couldn't even pull out. I was literally stuck in that pussy as I nutted up in that shit. Even after I had stopped stroking, she was still throwing it back until my shit finally went limp on her. I had to sit down because my legs felt weak as shit and I needed a Newport. While I say and smoked, she ran upstairs and came back with a rag.

After she wiped my stomach, my dick, and in between my legs she took the rag back upstairs and came back to join me on the couch. I knew that she wanted me to stay but I couldn't, and she knew why. So, as I fixed my clothes, she continued to sit there pouting. It was what it was, though, and she already knew that. So, after we hugged, I was out the door. I had left her with a kiss, though. Shit, that pussy was something serious, so she at least deserved that.

It took me twenty minutes to get back across town to the extended stay. I was dead tired, and that little fuck fest had only made it worst. Not to mention the fact that I had been up for some days with no break or a nap. Once I had parked, I snatched up everything and run upstairs. Jumping in the shower, I washed myself before I got out and dried off. I didn't even bother to put on any boxers because believe it or not I still wanted to fuck the wifey.

Pulling the covers back and seeing her laying there naked only stemmed it. She was laying on her side with her back facing me, so I got on the bed and slipped right inside her. She woke up out the gate and threw her two cents in as she threw it back at me. I got the feeling that she hadn't even been sleep for real. I didn't stop to ask her though. I just kept right on stroking until I nutted. I ain't last but fifteen minutes but made sure she got hers twice.

I didn't even pullout because as soon as I came, I wrapped my arms around her and was out. I had put my phone on vibrate but it didn't really matter because I wouldn't have heard it anyway because once I went to sleep, I was dead until I wake up.

Chapter Twenty - Ruga

I was ducked off in the backseat while Doc drove and white girl Cindy sat beside him. Crack smoke had the truck cloudy but I ain't give a fuck. I probably had a contact, but I couldn't tell because I was already high after having snorted closed to a gram. My nigga Joog was the one who had put me up on the bag and I had been in love with it ever since. That power Courage made a nigga do what needed to be done every time. We were going down Lathrop when I told Doc to spin through Biggs so I could see if anyone of them nigga was out there. As soon as we made the turn, I say Mils and got excited.

"Ey, pull up on dude right there and ask him for three for twenty." I ordered Doc as I pointed at Mils so he would know who I was talking about.

"For what? Don't you got crack?" Doc asked causing me to get Irritated instantly. I was already feeling some type of way, so all the question shit was only adding to my attitude.

"Man, just do what the fuck I told you!" I demanded as I threw a shell in the head. I ain't bring the Kay but I had my forty though. I watched as Doc pulled down and then stopped in front of the duplex where mills stood on the porch. I watched as Cindy lowered the window and stuck her head out. I knew that nobody could see me in the backseat because Doc had tinted windows on the truck that we were riding in.

"Hey, you got three for twanty? " She asked mispronouncing the word due to her country ass accent.

"Yeah!" I heard Mils answer before he made his way down the steps. I waited until he was halfway to the truck, and I couldn't wait any longer. My trigger finger was itching, and I wanted revenge so bad I could taste it. Dropping the window, I upped the pole and I saw his eyes get big before he turned to run while shooting blindly behind him. I had only let off ten shots when one of the bullets nipped my ear causing me to let up on the trigger and duck. By this time Candy was screaming and Doc was pulling off going way to fast. He almost flipped the truck when he made a left off of Briggs on to Holloway Street.

"Fuck, fuck!" I yelled in frustration because I was mad as hell that I had fucked up around and missed that nigga.

"Fuck hell! You gotta get the fuck out my shit!" Doc fired at me as he bent a right on Guthrie and then slammed on the brakes.

"Oh, word?" I asked him already mad as fuck that I had missed and now he was trying to kick me out his whip.

"Man, get yo lil young dumb ass out!" He repeated as he turned to look at me to let me know he was serious. I ain't even argue with his ass though. I just upped the pole and fired right in his face before I turned to Cindy and hit her ass too.

Chapter Twenty-one
- Yella

I had been sleeping for three days straight and my phone had been going crazy. If it hadn't been for Shannon, I would have missed a lot of cake. Luckily, I had her ass trained so she made it happen while I was out. Still, I knew that she wasn't me and anybody that had called after ten at night had been shit out of luck. I had over ninety missed calls altogether and I probably would have still been sleep if bae hadn't woken me up. She had sold everything that I had left but she didn't know that I had a whole half a brick in the ceiling. So, when I got up and pulled it down, she looked surprised and shocked. I didn't even bother to answer any calls until I had finished whipping up.

I made sure to call Mils back because he had been calling and texting me nonstop, but I already knew why because he had told Shannon when she slid through to get him right. That was the first thing that she had told me once I woke up, but I still wanted to hear it from him. I knew he had only given her the edited version and I needed to hear the real one. Once I had hollered at him, I jumped in the shower and threw on all black. I was out the door a minute later with Shannon right behind me carrying my book bag and dressed in the same color as me. I didn't even try to make her stay because I knew that he wasn't going for it. She knew what was going on, so she was going to make sure I ain't do nothing stupid. She just ain't know though, because if I ran into Ruga I was planning on leaving him wherever I saw him. Big facts! It wasn't just because we had that little beef shit going either. That nigga knew that we had been the ones who touched Joog and he exposed his hand because he had been in my inbox on Facebook popping shit. I ain't even respond to that nigga because for one, I wasn't about to be putting my business on social media. I ain't know if the little nigga was trying to set me up or what but I wasn't going for it.

It took twenty minutes for me to get to the hood and the first place I went was TeeTee's house because she claimed that she had five hundred dollar play for me and I wasn't trying to miss it. I didn't even what to see who she had waiting so I just pulled up and grabbed what she owed me. Once I had that I threw her some more work and pulled off. Fuck that trap! I let her make it because at the end of the day it didn't matter because it was gonna come back to me anyway. Bending the block, I pulled straight up on Mils and scooped him up so he could tell me again what he had already told me on the phone.

Word on the street was that Ruga killed Doc and Cindy right after he had tried to smoke Mils. I couldn't understand the way that little young nigga thought, for real. I couldn't do shit, but shake my head at the dumb shit Ruga was doing. Then, that's when I thought about JC because I hadn't seen or heard from that nigga since the day Joog got smoked. What was even more crazy is that he still owed me money which made the situation even more fishy.

"Yo, you ain't seen JC?" I asked Mils as I looked at him in the rearview mirror to catch his reaction to my question. I wanted to see if I was just tripping or if somebody else was feeling where I was coming from.

"Man, hell nah! That nigga been ghost since the other day!" He said before he made a crazy ass face added, "Then somebody told me that he smoking crack and shit!"

"What? Hell nah?" I said as I shook my head because hearing that caused me to think back to a couple times when I went behind that nigga in the bathroom, and it smelled like straight caine. At the time I ain't think nothing of it because where we had been was a crack house, so I figured that had been the reason. Now though I was starting to think otherwise.

"Hell yeah, Shadai told me that shit. She said Peewee told her!" Mils informed me, which was like music to my ears, because if Peewee knew, then all I had to do was ask to find out. In the meantime, I needed to find a way to get Shannon away from me so that me and Mils could go slide on Ruga. I was planning on laying on the fuck nigga this time because I wanted it done before something happened and he fucked around and snitched. Wasn't no telling who had seen him kill them two fiends, and I wasn't trying to be his way out.

Jumping on the highway, I sped to the Carolina Duke to serve Fran and send my bae on a mission to go and switch out the challenger. Being that her friend Shon had been the one to rent it for us, she couldn't even argue with me about it. She spoke her mind though before she got out the truck.

"I know you better do no dumb shit!" She told me as she looked at me with the serious face.

"Man, ain't nobody doing nun dumb!" I replied with a straight face that I knew she saw straight through me that bitch wasn't no dummy, and I knew that, but at the same time I wasn't about to tell her that we were about to go try to kill a nigga.

"Yeah, ain't whatever! What I need to get this time?" She asked me as I passed her a band to pay for the rental car.

"I don't know! If they got them new Nissan truck's get me one of them or a Tahoe or something!"

"Aight, be safe!" She said before she hopped out and let Mils sit where she had just been

"Aight and don't forget to take all that shit out of there before you switch out!" I instructed through the window before I backed out and slid off. I wasn't feeling Lucci at the moment, so I went to YouTube on my phone and pulled up that old Plies. I need my nigga to take me there because I was trying to catch a body. It didn't take us nothing but five minutes to get where we were going because our destination was only two exits away.

See, I knew that Ruga fucked with Narissa and I knew where she worked at through Shannon. Narissa did nails at a little shop off of Avondale Drive by where the old Kmart used to be. I also knew that she drove an Audi A4 that she had gotten at tax time and that it was silver in color. I didn't park right away when I whipped into the parking lot because I wanted to see if I saw her through the glass. Sure enough, she was there but I noticed that her car wasn't. Looking at my wrist, I peeped that it was only three in the afternoon. The sign on the door said that they closed at seven and it was Friday. Knowing that, I figured that Narissa would stay until closing time so that she could catch all the business she could. I knew enough about that bitch to know that she was about her paper. I also knew that if her car wasn't there then that meant that fuck nigga was driving it.

"We gonna slide back through at like six thirty! He gotta come get his bitch and this time I'm gonna put it to his forehead!" I promised as I slid off and shot to the hood. I needed to find JC and I needed to find Peewee as well so that I could pick his brain. As soon as I hit the block, I spent a couple corner's until I saw Peewee walking with Forest and Porsche. I pulled straight up on they ass and told Peewee to get in. As soon as he jumped in the back, I sped off and went straight in.

"Yo, you knew that nigga JC was smoking?" I asked him straight up acting like I already knew for sure. I was playing mind games but he ain't know it his mind was too clouded to realize it.

"Man!" was all he said but it was enough to let me know that it was the truth and not just a rumor that was going around.

"You ain't seen him, have you? That nigga owes me someone chicken and I need it ASAP!" I asked him as I bent a right on Liberty Street.

"Yeah, he at the rooming house on Driver with that ho Taylor! Her old stinking pussy ass!" He told me and then laughed before asking me for singing t put on his stem.

I told Mils to give it to him as I bent another right and pulled back up on Forest and Porsha. Peewee must've known he was being dismissed because he hopped out as soon as I stopped. I sped off as soon as the door closed and bent two right before I was on Driver and jumping out in front of the room house. I told Mils to sit tight while I went up in there to get the boy. I knew every crack head that lived in the rooming house so I knew it wouldn't be hard to locate his ass. The first person I saw was this little bitch named Trina that my brother Edward used to talk too that bitch wasn't shit but a jump off though and life had beat her down so bad that she was on that dog food now.

"Ey, Trina you know which room Taylor and JC in?" I asked her, getting straight to the point because I ain't really give a fuck how she was doing.

"Um, what the fuck, I look like map quest?" she asked snaking her neck as she looked up at me from where she sat on the porch steps. I started to smack the bitch, but I knew I would have to really beat her ass because that little bitch was with the bullshit. Bitch was still had because I told my brother that she let me fuck.

"Bitch, where the fuck they at? I asked again except this time I had pulled out a twenty dollar bill and was waving it in her face. I already knew that old dope fiend ass bitch would talk for that paper so that she could go cop a bag.

"I got your bitch! But they in my room." She snitched as she snatched the money out my hand.

"Shut up, bitch, you ain't got shit but some wack ass pussy!" I told her while stepping around her so I could slide through the door. I already knew where that bitch's room was, so I went straight to it and opened the door surprising the shit out of JC and Taylor. Out the gate I could see that they both high off that shit and geeking. I ain't even say nothing right away because I wanted to see what JC was gonna say. The caine must've had him stuck though because he wasn't saying shit.

"Muthafucka looking for you and you hiding smoking crack, right?" I finally said to him because I was tired of just standing there looking. He couldn't even give me no answer. I didn't know if it was because he was ashamed or rif it was because of the caine or if it was a little bit of both. Either way it pissed me off and made me step across the room in two strides and smack him with the pistol. I smacked Taylor next just because I felt like it.

"Arrghh what fuck you hit me for?" Taylor screamed causing me to throw the pistol in her face.

"Scream again, bitch!" I dared her as I backed up a step still pointing the gun at her. Once I saw that she wasn't gonna scream, I turned back to JC. "Where the fuck my cash, at nigga?" I asked him already knowing that he had probably fucked it up.

"My my my mama had to pay her car note so so so I let her hold s-s- some m-m-money I s-supposed to go pick it up when I g-g-get a r-r-ride!" He stuttered I knew he was lying but it was the perfect answer I needed him to say so I could get his dumb ass in the truck while he thought of another excuse.

"Well, come on let's go get it, cuz I gotta go get right!" I lied as I waved the gun towards the door to direct them in the direction, I wanted them to go. Didn't nobody move though and being that my patience had been ran out I was tempted to pop they ass right there. I knew if I did that though I would've had to pop Trina's dumb ass too.

"Yo, y'all muthafuckas can't hear?" I said get the fuck up and let's go! Next thing gonna happen ain't gonna be no talking. I'm gonna be shooting and JC you know how I'm coming so play with ya kids not me." I told them which got they ass to moving like I wanted.

Once they walked out with me behind them, I put my gun back up and followed them all the way to the truck Trina was still sitting on the porch watching but it was all good because I had a trick for that ass too.

Jumping back in, I sped off and headed towards the north to Cariage house and old farm. It took us twenty minutes to get there because I took the back way behind Braggtown. I was headed to the park in old Farm because I knew that wouldn't nobody be out there at this time. I pulled up and it was nearly deserted. The two car that were there were about to pull out which would leave us out there dolo. Perfect! It took about five minutes for them to go and as soon as they did, I made everybody get out. I whipped my shit back out so I could maintain order as Mils followed my lead without being told. I led the way into the park's restroom and then turned around to face Taylor and JC. Mills brought up the rear leaving them stuck in the middle.

"Y-y- yella why you doing this? I....." was all he out out his mouth before I shot him in it blowing JC brains all over his baby mama. As soon as he hit the ground, I tapped the trigger two more times before I upped on Taylor. I sent one at her and stretched her ass out right beside her nigga.

"Ey yo, hit both they ass so we can go!" I told Mils and he nodded before shooting both of them in the head. It was overkill but it was necessary in my eyes. Satisfied, I left back out the same way I had come with Mils behind me. I made sure to look around to see if anybody was around. When I saw that there wasn't, I jumped in the Benz, and we slid off. It was going on five thirty, which meant that we had an hour before we needed to be back at Narissa's job. I wasn't trying to miss my chance and I could tell that Mils was just as anxious as I was. Even though we both knew that Bandanna had been the one who smoked Joog, Ruga didn't and he was blaming us. I bent a couple corners to waste time and bae had texted a picture of the truck she had gotten. It was one of them new Dodge Ram's and it was black! I knew I was about to cut up in that and I told her to meet me back at Fran's room at seven thirty.

At 6:20, I started heading toward Avondale Drive. At 6:35, I was backing in a spot that gave me a clear view of Narissa and the parking lot. I saw that she was working on some bitch hands, so I started to roll me up a blunt to ease my mind. I was far from nervous believe me1 I had just caught two bodies and was about to catch two more, so I needed to get my mind right. By the time me and Mils had finished the blunt, I noticed that Narissa had finished with her client and was cleaning up here station. The time said that it was 7:10. Ruga was late! Another five minutes went by and still nothing. At 7:20, my baby called me to tell me that she was on the way to Fran's room but I stopped her and changed the time to 8:30. She started bitching but I wasn't paying her no mind. I wasn't going nowhere until this nigga pulled up. And just as soon as I thought it the shit happened in slow motion.

"There he go Mils! there he go!" I said excitedly as I gripped my fire. I watched he parked in s spot close to the door of the shop. Narrisa's car didn't have any tint on it, so I knew for sure that it was that nigga ruga driving. As soon as I saw the break light dim back to the regular ounces. I threw my door open and jumped out. Mils was with me and we both had left our door wide open. I crept up on the driver side and Mils the passenger. That nigga had the window halfway down listen to Youngboy as he busted a cigarillo down. He didn't even see it coming so I warned him.

"Slipping ain't you!" I said and then bit my lip as he looked up. By this time Mils had walked around to the front of the car and was aiming at the nigga through the windshield. I heard Narissa scream at the same time that I pulled the trigger. I knew his ass was gone for sure this time because I had put the pistol to his temple while Mils threw thirty shots through the windshield. I hadn't planned on killing Narissa buy that bitch knew my face, so I upped the pole and sent something through the glass that uncased the nail shop. I didn't know how many times I had hit her, but I saw the one that counted most when it left a hole in her forehead.

"Come on, nigga!" Mils yelled at me from the truck before he jumped in. At few second later I was spinning tires as I sped out of the parking lot. I jumped straight on the highway and went straight to Fran's room. I still had another two days with the truck, but I had decided to give that cracker his shit back early. Fuck that truck! Benz or not! It didn't fascinate me anymore because I had just used it to commit four murders. My baby pulled up thirty minutes after

I did, and we shot straight to the east to drop Mils off. Before he got out, I gave him another Ounce to go with what he had already and then pulled off. We were going down Liberty Street we I remembered something.

"Turn right here, bae." I told Shannon making her bend a right on Driver Street. Once I told her where to pull over at, I jumped out the truck and ran across the street. Walking through the door of the rooming house I went straight to Trina's room and knocked.

"Fuck you want?" She asked me as soon as she opened the door and saw it was me. She wasn't shit but four feet ten so I could see over her head and the room.

"How much you gonna charge me for some of that pussy?" I asked her once I saw that the room was empty and waiting for a nigga like me.

"Oh, now you want some pussy? Well since it was so wack earlier. " She said as she did the quotation sign with her fingers and a smirk on her face she added, "I'm gonna charge yo ass two hundred!"

"Aight! You ain't said nun slick to a can of oil." I shot back giving her the same smirk she had just given me.

"Okay, money first!" She demanded holding her greedy ass hand out.

"Damn, you don't trust me? here man!" I said as I counted out ten twenty dollar bills.

"Okay, how you want it?" she asked walking over to the couch.

"Bend yo ass over!" I ordered and watched as she did it. Standing behind her I yanked her pants down and then smacked that little ass causing her to let out a slight moan. She didn't even see it coming I grabbed a pillow off the couch and used it to push her head down. Pressing my gun to the fabric, I squeezed and watch as her stupid ass thoughts painted the seat of the couch.

I took the same two hundred I gave her and stuck that shit back in my pocket. I knew that didn't nobody hear the shot because the TV was up, and the pillow had muffled the sound. Still, I was cautious as I left to make sure nobody was watching me.

"Where we going now, bae?" Shannon asked me looking small as hell behind the wheel.

"Take me to the room!" I told her because my as was going back to sleep.

Chapter Twenty-two
- Rontay

Shit, I don't know why I ain't been jumped in the story because I am Yella's brother. I'm older than him by four months and two days. Poppa was a rolling stone because there were three boys and two girls including me. Edward was the oldest out of the boys and Yella is the baby. Both girls are younger than all three of us because our daddy had made them where he had come home from doing a dime.

I know like everybody else that Yella runs the east, but when his ass is asleep that when I get off. That's why I was pulling up on my uncle Peewee now because he had just hit me talking about, he had a mean play for a nigga. I had just bent a left on Gilbert and pulled up and parked across the street from Ms. Kathy's house. I really didn't want to be around this house because I knew that nigga Joog had just got stretched a few feet from where I was parked. I knew my brother was beefing with them or had been in the past, but last I checked that shit was dead. I knew that it couldn't have been Yella who did it, so I ain't even think to ask. I wasn't there to see Ms. Kathy or anybody that was at her house though Peewee was at the house. It was another spot where a lady in a wheelchair lived. Blowing the horn, I waited a few seconds before I saw the door crack. Peewee came out with some Mexican dude behind him. It wasn't no telling who this muthafucka here was, but I already knew Peewee wasn't gonna bring me no police, so I wasn't tripping.

"Wassup, nep nep?" He asked as soon as he jumped in the front seat. He left his door open as the Mexican stood close by watching us.

"Wassup, Peewee? What you go going on?" I wanted to know so we could do it and I could get the fuck off this hot ass street. I wasn't trying to get pulled on no humbug shit because I ain't have no license and I was dirty. I had dope and caine and I had a whole ounce of gas on me. On top of that, I wasn't in no rental. I was driving my own shit today. I had a little white Dodge Avenger with black and white twenty twos squeezed on it to match the car and tint.

"Shit you already know if I hit you it's some show nuff money!" He assured me chuckling before he continued.

"But check this out this, nigga, got two hundred and he got two five hundred dollar gift card for Walmart!"

"Shit, them card only go for half price!" I let it be known just in case Peewee thought he was about to finesse me.

"Nigga, I know that! what I wanna know is what you tryna give up for all that?" He asked as he gave me that look to let me know he was finessing the mego.

"I got you, Peewee!" I told him as I went in my bag and broke off a couple pieces until I eyed balled close to seven grams.

Before I gave it to him, though, I made sure to call the number on the back of the two cards to make sure that their balances said five. Satisfied, I gave Peewee the caine and watched him tuck like three grams before he jumped out. I couldn't do nothing but shake my head because I knew that he was keeping that for himself and was probably gonna get half of the other shit too. Them east Durham crackheads trip me out, for real.

Swerving off, I turned my shit back up so I could finish listening to that new Jeezy. I bent a left on spruce and then another left on Holloway. I pulled up at the Big Apple next because I needed some Dutch Master cigarillos. Soon as I pulled up that ho, Boosie ran up to my car begging me for a wake up. It was one in the afternoon, so I knew the bitch had been woke but I threw her like two dimes anyways. Running in the store, I saw that Brooke was at the counter giving Ali all her one's and five's so he could give her some big bills. I knew that she had stolen that idea from Yella because that what he always did. It was crazy how she had jumped ship and my brother but that wasn't none of my business. I already knew how hos do a nigga when he get locked up so the episode wasn't nothing but a played rerun.

"Wassup, Blacky?" She asked me once she saw me walking through the door. The bell on the door had announced my entrance and took away the element of surprise.

"Ain't shit, what's good?" I asked back smiling as I checked her little fine ass out. That bitch was bad for real and I knew I'd fuck if I ever got the chance. Her and her sister Morgan could get it.

"Nothing! Where yo ho ass brother at?" she asked me turning back around as she counted a handful of twenty dollar bills. I guess since she had been booming all of a sudden that she knew Yella wasn't around. That's the only time that anybody else eat because brah had shit sown up!

"I don't know where that nigga at. He probably asleep somewhere!" I said but I already knew he was sleep because I had already talked to Shannon earlier.

"Yeah, probably! His ass need to stay sleep to!" He said laughing as she left out going back outside where here little two door cobalt was parked. Once I got my rello's I slid back out the door also and posted up in the front so I could catch a couple sales. I ain't like Yella because I don't like being in the east all the time. I be in and out and all around because I like to keep moving. I wasn't trying to get caught standing still. Really though that dope is what had me bouncing around because I had plays all over the place. Durham, Raleigh, Butner, Creedmoor, and Henderson were some of my everyday stops. I was always on the road up and down the highway going here or there.

Shit, I had to make my own lane and take my own path. Even though I knew that I could get money with brah, it wasn't nothing like being the captain of your own ship.

I stayed posted up for like an hour before a play hit my phone. It was only for forty dollars, but every single dime added up, so I had to go snatch it. It took me ten minutes to shoot to the west end down Rosedale. This little nigga I fucked with waned two dubs of soft, so I pulled up on him and his homies. One of them looked like he was about to up the pole. Before he could whip out though, the nigga that had called me stopped him.

"Damn, ya boy was about to start hitting, huh?" I joked as I eyed the little nigga who had gripped on me. I didn't stare though, I just leek long enough to let the nigga know that if he had done what he started to do that it would've been a problem.

"Nah, he good! Shit just been going up round here lately, you feel me?" My trap explained as he passed me two tens, three fives and five one dollar bills.

"It all good, my nigga. Get at me, though, ya heard?" I told him as I passed him two fat ass dubs before I slid off. Ten minutes later, I was pulling up on Colfax where I lived at with my bitch Jody and her mama. Blowing the horn as I kept my foot on the break, I waited in the middle of the street until my bitch came out Jody wasn't really shit, to look at but I still loved her. I don't know if it was the head of nah, but I was stuck like a fly on a piece of duct tape. She kind of favored Oprah a little bit but she was shaped like a upside down pear. She was real muffin top and real freak. It took her ass almost five minutes to come out the crib and I think she took her time on purpose. That bitch had been blowing me up to come get her and then when I pulled up, she wanna drag her feet. It wasn't nothing new to me though because I knew she love to nitpick and go tit for tat. Her and Shannon were best friends which is how Yella and her got together.

"Damn, yo ass took ya time, didn't you?" The fuck!" I said with my face screwed up as I sped off. The sudden motion made her head snap back and smack the headrest. I was glad to because something needed to knock some sense into that bitch.

"Boy bye, I been waiting on yo ass to pull up for three hours and you act like you can't wait for me for two minutes. Fuck out of here with that shit for real." She shot back with her smart ass mouth. I ain't even say nothing else to her dumb ass because I ain't feel like arguing. Bitch wasn't making no kind of money but had all the lip in the world. Then wanted to wonder why a nigga be creeping with other hoes. Pulling up to the light by Hill top shore, I saw a black Dodge Ram bend the corner before it swerved over and stopped right beside me. I thought it was a hit until I looked up and saw that Shannon was leaning out the window smiling.

"Where the fuck you get that?" I asked curiously causing Jody to lean over to see who I was talking to.

"Hey bitch! What you doing? Where you about to go?" Jody asked quickly knowing that the light was about to turn green any minute.

"I'm about to go make this play on Dawkin for Yella and then Im going back to the room?"

"Oh, okay! Why yo ain't come get me? You riding around stunting and shit. Damn!" Judy went on until I cut in.

"Shit, let's switch for a little while, Shannon?" I suggested trying to squeeze my way up in that big muthafucka.

"Boy bye, you ain't about to get me jumped on and cussed out!" Shannon told me seriously as the light changed.

"Aight, well tell brah to hit me up ASAP!" I told her and then slid off before Jody could say goodbye. I heard Shannon blow the horn behind me as she went the opposite direction shit, even the horn on that big muthafucka sounded good.

"Damn, you could've let me say bye to my friend!" Jody fired at me with a little attitude. I turned that Jeezy back up and acted like I ain't even here her ass. I saw her looking at me all crazy out the corner of my eye though. Fuck her! I was tired of her ass, but like I said it was just something about her that wouldn't let me leave.

Chapter Twenty-three
- Shannon

I was feeling myself, for real. Ever since I had taken the Challenger back had the truck to myself. Yella hadn't even drove the muthafucka yet. I had some of everywhere too. Yella had been sleeping for almost two days but it was about time for him to get up though because I had a bone to pick with his ass. I had heard that somebody killed Ruga and Narissa at her job the other night. I don't know what it was, but something was telling me that my man had did that shit. then they had found two bodies in old Farm, and it turned out to be that boy JC and his baby mama. I knew that Yella had been looking for him and I was guessing the reason he couldn't find him was because he was dead. Shit was crazy as hell bit it wasn't my place to judge nobody or point fingers.

Pulling up on Dawkins, I parked and waited for CeeCee to come jump in the truck. I wasn't like Yella, so I wasn't about to get out and all that. Muthafucka wanted to get served they had to get they ass in. I didn't like this bitch CeeCee anyways because I had heard that she was trying to fuck my man. I wasn't tripping yet, but if I ever got solid proof best believe that ass was gonna get whipped. Wasn't no bitch gonna be smiling in my face and then stabbing me in my back and think Shannon wasn't gonna pop.

"Wassup, CeeCee?" I asked her as soon as she jumped in and close the door. That bitch had on a pair of black leggings, a multi-colored blouse, and some fruity ass Jays on. I couldn't even front, to be a crackhead that bitch kept herself up nice. She even had her hair done with a little knock off Gucci bag.

"No, girl, out here tryna get it!" She said with a smile and a tone that suggested that I should know where she coming from.

"I hear that! What you want, though?" I asked trying to hurry up and get the transaction over with. I wasn't with all that chit chat. Especially not with that ho right there.

"Give me something good for this!" She told me as she passed me a crispy ass blue face.

"But yeah, girl, you need to tell Yella to come through and holla at me ASAP for real!" She added as I got her shit together. When she said that shit though I paused and looked at her because I want to know what the fuck Yella needed to see her for when I was already before I wanted to know what the fuck Yella needed to see her for when I was already right there serving her ass. I guess my face said it all because before I could reach over and smack that bitch or say anything back, she cleared it up.

"Nah, I don't mean none like that I'm saying it's a lot of money over here and these lil boys that's over here ain't running it right so he could come and take this shit over easy!" She explained to me making me relax. I still had to take me a deep breath though because I had been a second away from being on that ass.

"Oh yeah?" How you know CeeCee?" I asked her as I gave her what she paid for. Shit, I had an idea in my head so I needed to know what she knew. I was getting gored sitting up in that hotel room all the time.

"Cuz I done been fucking with them!" She said with a smirk, and it made me think if the rumors about her and Yella were true.

"Well, I'm gonna talk to him and see if he'll put me out here. If he do, you gonna show me right?" I questioned her to see if she was willing to work with me of if she was after my man.

"Yeah, girl! But you need to let Yella come through and put his food down around here first because these lil niggas do get stupid." She told me but I had already figured as much.

"Oh, you already know that nigga ain't gonna, play but I'm gonna holla at him though. Let me get up out of here because it about time for me to wake him up anyways." I said ready to go.

"Aight, but don't forget!" She said hopping down.

"Aight, CeeCee! Close the door so I can go!" I said as frustration creeped into my voice. I didn't have to tell her twice so as soon as the door shut, I sped off and headed for the hotel.

I had been gone since early that morning and I knew it was time for me to check in. Yella was unpredictable and it wasn't no telling how long he would sleep or nah. He was the only nigga I knew that could stay up a week straight and take a three hour nap and get right back up and go for another week. When it came to trapping, Yella was a fucking beast for real. He scared me sometimes though because I knew when he got tired, he'd fall asleep anywhere. I knew this because I had to wake him up a couple times when he had been riding and his ass had fallen asleep at the red light. Now that's just crazy and that's when you know you going to hard.

It took me like twenty minutes to get to 15-501 but I didn't go straight to the room because I had places a order over the phone. I knew my man would be hungry when he woke up so that's why I was pulling up at mayflower. I knew what to order him because we both always got the same thing. The only thing different was that he liked a baked potato with his meal, and I preferred the corn on the cob. Being that i had called the order in, I didn't have to wait when I got there because it was ready.

Five minutes later, I was pulling up to the Extended Stay. I made sure to grab all the work and money before I got out with the food, walking through the door, I saw that Yella was already up and looking at me like the fucking Devil. By the way he was looking I knew that he was rubbed. I figured he was mad because I had taken his phone with me like I always did.

"Damn, where the fuck yo ass been at all day?" he started right up as I placed the food on the table and then handed him the money and the work.

"That's where I been! And how long you been up?" I asked him after I saw that he was fully dressed with his shoes on.

"I been up for a minute!" He answered snatching his phone out my pocket where it had been sticking out. I had on some woman's Levi's so the pocket weren't that deep.

"You hungry?" I asked him already knowing that he was.

"Yeah, you went and saw CeeCee? It say she called almost hour ago." He said telling me what I already knew.

"Yeah, I want and saw ya lil girlfriend!" I told him just to get under his skin. I knew it pissed him off when I called her that and the look he gave me told me that my words had hit their target.

"What she talking about?" he asked as he took the box of seafood that I was handing him.

"She said you need to go take that little block over cuz it be doing numbers. I told her I would see if you would let me do it and I was gonna get her to help me!" I said throwing it out there. I was trying to shoot my shot forreal because I was tired of watching love and Hip hop all day. I needed something to do and since he wouldn't let e work then traping was the next best thing. Plus it would help us get more money a little bit faster.

"Oh yeah?" he asked with his eyebrow raised and a smirk on his face.

"You think you ready for all that?" He continued questioning me between bites of food. By the way he was fucking his food up a muthafucka could tell he hadn't eaten in days.

"Man, hell yeah I'm ready. I been watching you, so I know what to do!" I assured him with a straight face because I needed him to see that I was forreal! I knew that shit wasn't no game, so I had to let him see that I knew it.

"You sure?"

"Yes, bae!" I said starting to whine because I knew that it would make him do it. I always got my way when I did it so I was using all the tricks I could.

"I hear you!" He told me and I knew that meant that I had his blessing. That's when I remembered all the other shit I had to ask and tell him.

"Oh, bae you know JC got killed?" I asked him as I looked at him. He looked at me with surprise written across his face, but he didn't say shit, so I continued.

"Yeah, they found him and his baby mama in old farm!" I said before I switched topics. "They say Ruga and Narissa got killed to!" I told him what I knew he already knew in a tone that told him that I knew he already knew.

"Oh yeah?" He asked with his eyebrow raised again. He was playing dumb, and I knew it.

"Did you do that shit?" I asked him and he looked at me like I was the one that was crazy.

Chapter Twenty-four
- Yella

There wasn't no way I was about to admit that I had murdered Ruga and Narissa. Shannon had me fucked up if she thought that shit for real. Even though I knew she probably already figured that I had been the one who had done it, that still didn't mean that I had to confirm it. The less people that knew the better my chances were if I were to ever get picked up for it. I had smoked five muthafuckas in a matter of two weeks and for of them had died for being witnesses to some shit. I wasn't trying to have to ever do nothing to hurt Shannon unless it involved sticking my dick up in her. Even then, I still wouldn't be hurting her because pain is pleasure. I know it pissed her off that I didn't answer her question but some shit she didn't need to be knowing.

As soon as we ate, I got up and lit me a Newport. I saw that she had made close to six bands, and it made me smile. Going to the closet to check my stash, I quickly counted how many zips I had left. I was down to the last ten so I knew I would have to go holla at the plug in another two or three days. I also know that we had close to seventy thousand sitting in the room and I didn't like that. Which is why I made may help me count everything we had except for the change. I took it all and that included pennies and electronics. I had three of those office water jugs full of change, and I had a drawer full of rolled up quarters, dimes, and gold dollars.

Once we finished counting it blew my mind because the total came to seventy nine five. That meant that I had overlooked almost a whole ten stacks. I really ain't have no idea where that shit came from, but I wasn't about to complain about it. Instead, I put the fifteen that I owned the plug to the side, and I added another thirty to it before I threw all of that into the same bag that he had given me. Once I did that, I took forty five hundred and put it in my pocket. The other thirty I gave it to Shannon for her to put inside the Lexus outside because I was about to move my shit and park it at my mama house. I also had her take the guns I got from Jim, along with a few more, and place them in the car as well. I was planning on moving tomorrow because I didn't feel comfortable there no more.

It took us an hour to get shit done because we came back for the Chevy. I didn't take that to my house though because I was on some more shit. Instead, I pulled up at Rim Tyme and dropped that bitch off. My bae was plain Jane, but the paint was already wet because I had brought it like that. Once I picked out the Rims that I wanted and they told me how long it would take for them to be shipped to their store, I left them with the keys and then dipped. We had been riding for close to thirty minutes when Shannon came out the blue and started talking.

"But why we gotta keep wasting money on these room when we got more than enough to get us a spot? I mean when we started out shit was rough, so we had to. Why not get a crib in the cut?" she asked me as I drove towards the south side to go holla at CeeCee. I didn't answer right away, because I wanted to let what she was saying asking

"Where, though? It can't be anywhere, and it can't be around nobody that's gonna be all up in our shit either!" I said finally as I looked at her real quick to see what she'd say next. She had my full attention because we were now stuck at the light by North Carolina Central.

"Yeah, I know!" She agreed but still yet to say where though.

"And it gotta kinda be close to everywhere I roam and get money so don't be thinking about no out of town shit." I said just in case she started getting any ideas about that.

"So, what you want me to start looking?"

"Yeah, but you can do that later! In the meantime, though we still moving tomorrow!" I let it be known as I sped off through the light. A few minutes later I pulled up on CeeCee at the rooming house on Linwood. Once she jumped in the backseat, I turned around so I could holla at her.

"What up with it?" I asked her as I looked her in the eye. We were about to discuss business, so I wasn't playing with it.

"She ain't tell you?" She asked answering my question with a question.

"Yeah, and I'm asking you now is this shit legit or nah? Because you know how I'm coming so I need to know everything down to the littlest detail. I need to know who, what, and where!" I said running that shit down to her. She ain't have to know that I had already been plotting on coming through. I had already peeped that Dawkins was goldmine as well as Linwood because of all the rooming houses that occupied that street.

Once CeeCee gave me the rundown about everything, I dismissed her with the promise that we would be back when the sun went down. I wanted to come through then because I knew that that's when I would get to see who was out there and who was just in the way. I wanted to go scoop up Peewee and forest so I could bring them over there with me. Mils knew how to run shit so he could use anybody to watch the strip. I needed my runners with me so that they could mingle and so I could also have somebody over there that I could trust other than Shannon and CeeCee. I was planning on taking over Dawkins myself. I was gonna let Shannon and CeeCee do their thing on Linwood.

I pulled up on my little nigga Mils next to chop it up with him and to see where his head was at. Baby boy had caught four bodies with me so I wanted to make sure he was alright. That little nigga wasn't nothing but nineteen, but I knew that the street made adult out a child real quick.

"What good, baby boy?" I asked him after I had hopped out the truck I ain't Shannon all in my mouth, so I had gotten out. I was crazy because I hadn't been on the block in a minute. I had been swinging through in the whip but that wasn't the same thing as being posted.

"Yeah, I'm good! You?" He asked as he lit a cigarette and gave me a look as if he was worried about me. It made me laugh because he was like me in a lot of ways.

"Yeah, baby boy, I'm good!" I told him still laughing which made him smile.

"What's so funny?"

"Nah, it ain't nun I'm just laughing at something that happened earlier I was just thinking about!" I lied as I lit a cigarette on my own. We didn't say nothing for a minute. Both of us were lost in our own thoughts as we enjoyed our cigarettes.

"You know the word is they saying Ruga and his bitch got hit by some niggas?" Mils finally said after he had flicked the butt from his Newport.

"Oh yeah?" I asked him as I noticed Shadai walking up with a tight ass body suit on. That shit was so tight that I could see her pussy lips poking through the fabric. I didn't stare though because I knew that bae was hawk.

"Yeah! They say they claiming it all on Facebook and shit." He said laughing before Shadai jumped in our conversation to get her fix. I let Millz go ahead and serve her though as I jumped back up in the truck. I didn't pull off though because I still wanted to holla at him.

"You good on the work? Cuz I'm gonna be in the south tonight so I ain't gonna really be mobile like that!" I asked him once he had finished making the trap.

"I got like a fourteen left."

"Aight, take this! It should get you through the night. If not, you gonna have to find a ride to come pull up on me." I explained to him as I handed him two zips through the window. Tucking it in his draws he said.

"Aight, I should be ready for you in the morning!"

"That's what's up! You been saving ya money?" I wanted to know because it was about time he got some wheels to move around in. All that walking shit wasn't cool and I knew his feet had to be tired of his ass.

"Little something!" he said smirking as two fiends walked up looking.

"Aight, baby boy, I'm up out of here I'll holla!" I said tapping the horn as I slid off and bent a left up Holloway. I had to go find Peewee and Forest.

Chapter Twenty-five
– Yella

As soon as the sun dropped, we hit Dawkins like we were supposed to be over that bitch. The first thing I did was give everybody a free rock to let them know what it was hitting for and to show them that I had it. The niggas that were over there hustling were in the way for real and I knew that it wouldn't be long before I pushed they ass to the side. I wasn't gonna start no shit though until somebody brought it to me. Once that happened then I was gonna go ahead and show my ass like a magic city stripper. I had a feeling that it would be sooner than later though because one nigga in particular had been watching me ever since we showed up.

I had already gotten the nigga's whole DNA and MO through this fiend named Michelle. Michelle was just like Peewee was for my block. She was all the way in the mix. She had told me that old boy went by the name Lil EJ and he kept a gun on him all the time. She also told me that he was really more bark than bite. Long story short I had to step to him to see what was up and where his mind was at because I wasn't really with all that staring shit.

"Ey fam, let me holla at you right quick!" I said as I walked up on him. I wasn't aggressive with it, but I did say it with enough force to let him know what I wasn't intimidated either.

"What we need to holla about?" He asked with a attitude so I could already tell that the conversation probable wasn't gonna go right. Before I continued, I turned to look at Shannon who was standing beside CeeCee. I didn't have to use words to let her know to take CeeCee and take a little walk. I wasn't worried about nobody trying them because I had let my baby being the play toy that I had got for her a while back. Even still, Peewee knew that he was her designated babysitter so him and forest fell in step behind them.

Once they had started walking, I turned back around to face EJ so that we could finish talking!

"Now like I was saying I was tryna holla at you so I could find out why you keep watching my every move like you the Feds or something?" I asked him with a mug on my face which was a compete transformation the way I had originally came off.

"Cuz nigga, you all out here like you supposed to be! You ain't from over here, my nigga!" He said which made me bust out laughing.

"Nigga, and you not either. You from Lib and you over here because you can't go back there!" I shot back at his ass. As soon as Michelle had told me who he was I jumped on the phone about him. Shit I even knew who his bitch was already. This nigga was playing with the right one.

"Fuck you talking about, nigga? I can go back to Lib!" He said but I could hear it in his voice that I had hit a soft spot.

"Man, I don't give a fuck about all that. My thing is that I'm gonna get my money over here and if you got a problem with that then let it be known so we can go ahead and die behind it." I told his ass straight up as I stared him down and watched and waited to see if he was gonna try and reach on me. He didn't though, instead he turned and walked off. I should've shot his ass right then, but it was way too many witnesses watching for me to do that.

I knew his bitch ass was coming back.

Shannon and them did a loop around the block. They walked up a few minutes after EJ had left. We went back to doing what we had been doing but I kept my eyes and ears open still. At two o'clock I sent Shannon and CeeCee to the Waffle House to get the team something to eat. As soon as they pulled off, it wasn't a whole five minutes later when three niggas walked around the corner speed walking. I already knew who it was because they had just walked past Forest. Just like in the east we were using the walkie talkies and I had him posted around the corner.

I didn't wait for them to up on me first because I already knew what it was. I had fifty shot the ass because the forty had a drum on it. I sent like ten at them off rip and I hit one of them in the arm making him drop whatever he had in his hand. When he tried to pick it up, I started back up with the thunder and kept squeezing. EJ and the other one turned and left they nigga as he ducked and ran behind an old pickup truck that was parked near the corner.

"Peewee, get that gun!" I hollered as I took for after them. I guess the nigga that was hiding heard me coming so he took off before I could get him. Once I made it around the corner, I saw him dipping between two houses but EJ and the other one were still running in the middle of the street. I upped the pole again and tried one last time to drop something but missed.

Fuck! I said to myself as I looked at my gun to see that it was stuck on ugly. I wasn't tripping about the bullets though because I had extra drum inside of the book bag that Peewee wore on his back. Shit was quiet after that and after about a hour standing in the shadow, I realized that the police weren't coming.

"Boy, you see how them niggas run? Tryna come back fakin and almost got smoked out there!" Peewee said laughing as he stood in the crowd with the rest of the fiends. I was standing across the street in the cut, but I could still hear his ass over there carrying on. After my baby had come back with the food, I sent her and CeeCee over to Linwood just in case them nigga wanted to double back. I was definitely planning on pull on EJ sooner rather than later because I wasn't about to be walking on no eggshells worried about if he was gonna try me or not. That's why I was on Facebook now as I stood posted.

The traffic had kind of slowed down so the tricks weren't spinning the block as much. I wasn't tripping through because I knew that the city stood still between two and three. That gave me time to jump in EJ's girl's inbox after I saw that her ass was online. Me and her had been flirting with each other on the book way before I had pushed on Dawkins, but I had been hitting her ass with the curveball because I knew she was a thot. Now though, I was trying to see about that bitch so I could lay up my trap. It didn't take much though, because just like that I had her ho ass sending me pictures of that pussy. I ain't even gotta lie, that shit had me ready to run over there but I ain't want to seem too thirsty. I wasn't trying to get hit with the triple cross moving too fast. For all I knew, I could've been getting set up even though I didn't think so. Like I said, me and that bitch had been on some more shit way before now. I knew her through my cousin Darrin's baby mama because they hung in the same circle.

When three o'clock rolled around, shit started jumping again just like I knew it would. Then my brother pulled up to make a dope store but once he saw that it was popping her packed and got out. That nigga didn't even see me, so I told Forest and Peewee not to say nothing because i was about to scare the shit out his dumb ass. I waited until he was in the middle of selling another bag, and I crept across the street on his ass. Before he knew what was happening, I pressed my fire into his back and disguised my voice.

"Yeah, nigga run that shit!" I said forcefully trying not to laugh, Peewee and forest were both hiding their laughter while everybody else thought that shit was serious.

"Man, goddamn! I knew I shouldn't have got out!" My brother said scolding himself for getting caught slipping. I burst out laughing because I couldn't hold it no more. That nigga was funny as fuck.

"You was scared as hell!" I said causing him to turn to turn around after he recognized my voice and heard me laughing.

"Man, why the fuck you playing? I started to up on yo ass!" He said with his face screwed up which made me laugh at his ass even harder.

"Nigga, stop capping, you won't about to do shit but get stripped!" I told his ass.

"Aight! Fuck you doing over here" He asked me pulling out half a blunt from inside his pack of Newport's.

"Handling business, nigga! I'm about to take this little shit over!" I told him because I was fully confident that I was gonna do it. "You everywhere, ain't you?"

"Tryna be! You strapped?" I asked him as I took the blunt he was passing me.

"Yeah, why?"

"I was just asking because I had to up on that nigga EJ earlier!" I explained before I passed his shit back.

"Word? What EJ? From Lib?" he asked me as he took the blunt back.

"Yeah! Nigga ain't like what I told him so he tried to come back with his homies but I started shooting before they could try anything!"

"Oh yeah? You stay in some shit, boy!" He said telling me what I already knew. I couldn't help it if trouble always found me. While we were standing there my phone beeped in my pocket, so I pulled it out to check it. I had a message on the book from EJ's bitch. She was tying her best to get me to come through. I guess that little nigga wasn't fucking her right. I would, though!

"Ey, Peewee!" I called as I sold my phone back in my pocket.

"Yo?" he hollered back walking towards me with that stupid ass grin on his face. You could always tell when Peewee was really fucked up because he couldn't stop smiling.

"Check this out, I'm about to go make this move right quick so you and forest hold shit down for a minute!" I told him as I handed him a bag with like twelve grams in it.

"Aight, I got you!"

"Don't get missing, muthafucka!" I shot over my shoulder as me and Rontay made over way to where we were parked.

"Damn, I should've known yo ass was out here when I saw this truck. I saw Shannon driving that bitch earlier!" Rontay told me as he hit the unlock button on his key remote.

"Oh, word? Where you saw her at?" I asked just to see if she had been out of bounds somewhere.

"At the light by the Hill Top store. She pulled up on me and Jody!"

"Aight! I'm about to slide though brah, get at me later!" I told him and then jump up in the truck. A minute later, I was pulling up on Linwood to check on Shannon and CeeCee. Once I did that, I was in traffic cutting up to that new lil Durk. I already knew where I was going because ole girl had already told me she lived in Bay creek with her sister. Sis was out of town, so I guess that why she was so anxious. It took me fifteen minutes to cut across town before I made a left off Leon Street and then a right into Bay Creek. I did a couple laps around the parking lot and complex just to make sure that I wasn't walking into a set up. Satisfied, I parked and then hopped out. I made sure I had one in the head just in case and I grabbed the shit I would need to roll up a couple blunts as well.

"Damn, nigga, it's about time. I finally got yo ass to come fuck with a bitch, huh?" She said all loud and ghetto as I walked up the step to third floor. She was standing in the door wearing a pair of booty Shorts that looked like they were painted on a black sports bra that barely contained her big ass titties. Her stomach was flat, and her feet were small but pretty. Her hair was in one long braid, but I could tell that she had a sew in. She was looking like a ghetto Maliah and I was wondering why I hadn't been slid through. Timing was everything though and I was there now, so fuck it.

"What's up?" I asked her as I bent down to give her short hug. She wasn't but five feet if that.

"Mmmmm, whatever!" she said pushing me playfully as she stepped back to let me in. " I hope you got some tree!' She added as she closed and locked the door behind me.

"Stay with it!" I assured as I made myself comfortable on the black leather couch that rested against the wall.

"Huh roll up!" I told her as I pulled my weed out along with a pack of rella's and sat it one the couch beside me.

"Where you was at when I was sending you them pictures?" She asked me smiling after she had sat down beside me to roll up.

"In the trenches getting to it." I told her as I took my strap off my waist and stuck it in between the seat cushion. She eyed the gun when she saw it but didn't say nothing. I knew she was a hood bitch, so she was used to being around fire.

"Probably laid up with one of yo bitches!" She said as she sprinkled gas through one of the Rellos.

"Nah, I would tell you if I was cuz you ain't nobody to lie to!" I told that bitch straight up.

"Oh, that how you feel?" She asked me like she had a attitude.

"Come on, man, don't do that cuz it ain't like that I'm just saying! I quickly answered trying to put a Band-Aid on the way I had just cut her with my word.

"It's like that. But I like that though cuz at least you ain't lead a bitch on and shit." She told me before she sealed the blunt with her luscious lips that were shined with gloss. I noticed she had a lil him mole and that shit just made her look even more sexy.

"What about you? Why you ain't call ya man instead of me?" I wanted to know I wanted to get as much info as I could.

"Cuz that nigga a dub!" She said straight up and then lit the blunt. " You don't know Lil EJ?" she asked me as smoke came through her nose.

"I know of him!" I answered nonchalantly. I wasn't about to tell her about the little situation we had because I didn't know she would take it. I knew bitches would say anything when they mad at they nigga but deep inside don't even mean it. Woman just be emotional and impulsive like that sometime.

"Yeah, anyway he be tryna play me like I'm stupid like he get it like that. He just don't know." She said passing me the blunt and then used the same hand to caress my dick through my pants. That shit was feeling good to and she had to know it since my shit was growing in her hand.

"Damn, you working with something, ain't you?" She asked as she continued to jack me through my jeans.

"You tell me!" I said as I unbuckled my belt and then slid my jeans down just enough to free myself. I guess she didn't want to smoke no more because as soon as my dick was out she started topping me off. She wasn't playing with it either. That bitch was making all the sound effects and everything like she was shoot a movie. I had to make her back up off if because she had me about to bust already. That bitch was dangerous for real.

"Mhm! That's how a real bitch suck dick!" She bragged laughing as she came out her bra and reached for the blunt. Once I passed it to her, I leaned over and put my mouth on her right nipple and sucked it real hard before I flicked my tongue across it real fast like I was eating pussy. I loved titties and hers were perfect.

"Ahh shit! That's my spot!" She told me as I made a circle with my tongue around her nipples. I was going back and forth from the left to the right as I squeezed them shit together using both hands. I Guess she couldn't take it no more because she out the blunt out and then forcefully pushed me back onto the couch as she stood up and then came out her shorts. Even though she had to peel them off it didn't take her long to do it. I didn't have no condom or nothing, but I didn't give a fuck. I watched her as she climbed in my lap and lowered herself onto my dick. That pussy was super wet, but it was tight as hell like she hadn't been fucked in minutes. She didn't even start slow either.

As soon as she had me all the way inside her, she went crazy. She was riding me like I was the last piece of dick on earth, so I had to grab ahold to that phat ass to gain some kind of control. When she same down I humped up giving it to her like she was giving it to me.

Our skin made music as we fucked like savages. She wasn't a screamer, but she did let a nigga know when she was coming. As soon as she did, I flipped her over and started digging in her with both of her legs pushed together ass I held her ankles with on hand. I was spanking that ass with the other as I kept the same speed that she had started. I was putting on a show because I needed this bitch to be wide open fr a nigga. When she told me that she was about to cum again I started fucking her even harder. Once I knew she came, I dropped her legs and pulled out.

"Turn that ass around and took that shit!" I told her as I came all the way out my clothes so I could move how I wanted to. Once she did, I told her to do I jumped right back in it. She was throwing that ass like a pitcher to first base, and I was loving the view. She had a pretty ass, and that shit was soft like newborn baby skin for real, I didn't last but another ten minutes because that pussy was the truth. Once we finished, I lit the blunt back up as I leaned back on the couch.

"I ain't never been fucked like that, yo!" She admitted as she play with my dick trying to get it to stand back up. I had to look at my watch to peep the time because I couldn't stay ghost forever. If I was gonna jump back in it again, I would have to harry up.

"You give up?" I asked her before I hit the blunt real hard and then put it out. I already knew what she was going to say before she even answered.

"Nah! I'm tryna go again!" She admitted looking up at me.

"Put it in ya mouth, then!" I told her as I gripped her ponytail and guided her head to where I needed it to be.

Chapter Twenty-six
- Shannon

Boy, this trapping shit was the truth. I felt like I was Yella my damn self because I didn't even want to leave. I was always fussing at his ass now look at me. It was going on five o'clock and this bitch CeeCee was steady bringing trap after trap. I guess it had a lot to do with the free rock she got for every sic scores she brought me. I knew I had done gave that hoe like fifty dimes already. I wasn't tripping though because that was my bitch. Yeah that's right I said it. I was actually starting to like CeeCee because that bitch knew how to go find cash. We had been talking and I got a better understanding of her as a person. That bitch had been through some shit and I probably would've been smoking to if it were me. I wasn't gonna put her business out there though because if she wanted muthafuckas to know then shed tell them.

Peewee had just hit me on the walkie talkie to tell me that him and a trap were walking around to Linwood because Yella still hadn't get back yet. In the back of my mind, I was wondering where the fuck he was at but I was too occupied with getting to the money. I'd give his ass another thirty minutes before I start blowing his phone up and acting crazy.

"Wassup, Peewee?" I asked as he walked up with two people. It had taken them five minutes to get to me and now that they were here, I thought I recognized the couple for somewhere.

"I told you I was bring you a play!" He said to me like I was being slow or something.

"Boy, shu,t the fuck up I know that I'm tryna figure out what they want!" I shot back a little irritated. I was kind of sleepy too! Peewee was about to get cursed the fuck out playing with me.

"Let me get a fifty niecy! You know me, right? You done been with Yella when he came to see me. I stay behind the Village!" She explained which help me remember. She was the one that had them big ass Rottweilers in her yard that always tried to jump in the car through the window and shit.

"You got that money from what Yella left you?" I asked Peewee after I had served the Trap. His ass was about to try and walk off until I said something.

"Oh, yeah, yeah, yeah, hear!" He said acting as he handed me the money. I thumbed through it right then so I would know exactly how much it was.

"Yella should be on his way back so I guess just keep bringing them around here because he ain't tell me to give you none, so I don't know!" I told him as I tucked the money in my back pocket away from the rest of what I had. I didn't want it to get mixed up just in case it wasn't right, and Peewee was on some funny shit. He got grimy every now and then, so I had to keep that in mind and stay out the center of his bullshit.

"Damn, where the fuck is this nigga at?" I asked myself as I saw CeeCee coming up the sidewalk with another muthafucka. I had done been online looking for us a crib too. Shit I was trying to show is ass to get his opinion. "He got a few more minutes though!" I told myself as CeeCee got closer.

Chapter Twenty-seven
- Yella

I had to jump in ole girl's shower before I left because I smelled like straight pussy for real. By the time I left her crib, it was ten after five and I knew that the sun was about to start coming up in a few more minutes. I could already hear the birds chipping and shit as I walked to the truck. I pushed the remote start from the steps so the Ram's system could he heard as well. I had already rolled me a blunt before I peeled but I waited until I got in before I lit it so that I could hot box the truck and get the soap smell up off me. By the time I made it to Fayetteville Street I was blitzed out my mind. Busting a left on Linwood I pulled straight up on Shannon and CeeCee as some young nigga stood close by talking to them. Before they even realized it was me, I was already jumping out.

"Fuck y'all got going on?" I wanted to know as I made my way around the front of the truck. I sized the nigga up out the gate like I just knew I was like that for real.

"I ain't got none going on, bae, he with her!" Shannon spoke up quickly cleaning shit up because she knew what time it was.

"Aight!" I replied relaxing because my shoulder had been tight, and my chest had puffed up full of air. I still didn't like that nigga being that close to my bitch though.

"He good, Yella, he with me! This my little boyfriend." CeeCee told me which made me look at her and then him with the crazy face. Little nigga must ain't know she was a ho.

"I know what you thinking, homie but I don't care about that. We all still people at the end of the day ya feel me?" That little nigga explaining. He ain't have to explain shit to me though because I really didn't give a fuck.

"Aww, that's why I love you!" CeeCee said before gave him a kiss on the lips that turned into them tonguing each other down. That shit almost made me roll on the sideway, for real. It wasn't no tell how many dicks CeeCee had done sucked in the last twenty for hours. That little nigga was nasty for that shit I didn't give a fuck what nobody said. I looked at Shannon and her dumb ass was smiling at they like she was watching a episode of love of love and hip hop or something.

"You about ready?" I asked her because I was trying to go ahead and move our shit out the room while it was early.

"Is you gonna leave something out here with CeeCee?"

"Is you gonna leave something out here with CeeCee? I thought this was yo block, Shannon?" I asked her before I walked back towards the truck without waiting on an answer. A few minutes later she got in beside me and I sped off and bent a circle back around to Fayetteville Street. A minute later, I was pulling up on Peewee and Forest. I left them with something I slid and headed for the highway.

It took us an hour to get there and get everything loaded. We had a room booked across town at another Extend Stay on 55/54. It took us another thirty minutes to get checked in and to get everything put up before I let her take a quick shower. While she was doing that, I was looking at my stash debating with myself about whether I would run out or if I had enough to last me another day. I was down to the last seven and being that I was on a new block I didn't know what kind of numbers it did yet. What I did know was that it couldn't possibly do more numbers than the east, so I decided to wait it out. First thing the next day though, I knew I'd have to go see my man's.

"Bae, I meant to tell you that I think I found some places!" My baby told me as she came out the bathroom ass naked.

"Oh yeah? Where at?" I asked as she bent over in front of me to grab an outfit out of one of her bags. I couldn't help myself, so I ran my tongue right up her ass crack causing her to jump and squeal with surprise.

"Boy, you better stop playing!" she said laughing as she punched me in the arm. I let her live though because I didn't want to get nothing started. We need to be on our way back out the door as soon as possible.

"It's a couple spots in the same area by Fayetteville Street and a spot up 98 past Turnkey and Rochelle!" She said as she stepped into her underwear.

"What the one on 98 look like and how much it cost?" I asked as I lit me a Newport and took a long pull.

"It's right and they talking about twelve hundred a month." She told me which was music to my fucking ears. Call me cheap or whatever but twelve hundred was good and it was on 98 so I knew it had to be ducked off in the low key spot.

"Aight, when they office open or whatever call and see what's up!" I told her as I took another pull. "Which one though?"

"We need to be looking at 98 first! I like how that shit sounding!" I let it be known as I watched her continue to get dressed. Ten minutes later we were back in traffic when my phone rang. It was

Bandanna so I answer out the game because I hadn't seen him or talked to him since that Joog incident.

"Wassup, nigga? You been hiding ain't you?" I asked him as I bent a right or Liberty Street. I was headed to Tater Bread so I could grab us something to eat before we went back to the south.

"Nah, never that, my nigga! What up, though? What you got going?"

"Shit! Same old, same old, out here bending a few blocks. You up early as shit that ain't like you!" I said peeping the time on the console in the truck. It was barely eight.

"Brah, I ain't even been to sleep. I been fucking with this little bitch all night! I started to pull up on you!"

"Where you at?" I asked him as I pulled up in front of Tater Bread.

"I'm in Durham, nigga. I been down here since yesterday!"

"Word? You in the city and you ain't pull up on real nigga?" I asked not believing it because that wasn't lie my nigga at all.

"Brah! When I say this little bitch a fool ain't lying!" He explained which let know but it still didn't sit right with me because anytime he came to the city or even close to it, he called me.

"What's her name? She know me?" I asked him making Shannon look at me with the stank face. I ain't care though because I had to know who the hell he was talking about.

"Just chill!" I mouthed to her shaking my head to let her know it wasn't nothing like that. She still was giving me the look, though, but I didn't give a fuck.

"Nah, she say she don't know you. I showed her yo Facebook page and all. Her name Precious, but her Facebook name is Black Barbie."

"Man, get the fuck out of here you talking about Precious Boyd. That bitch know who the fuck I am she done suc..." I had to catch myself because I had almost slipped and said some shit.

"Man, that ho know me she probably just aint wanna run you off." I added as I peeped Shannon watching me out the corner of her eye.

"Oh, word?" These hos ain't shit!"

"Tell me about it!" I said as I pulled out a twenty dollar bill and handed it to her as I nodded towards the building. She already knew what iI wanted so I didn't have to tell her.

"You ain't gotta hide and talk I don't care!" She said before slamming the door.

"Where you at?" Bandanna asked me making the speakers crackle a little.

"About to get something to get than go post up!"' I told him as I turned the volume down a little. I had my phone bluetoothed to the truck, so it was like talking on speaker phone.

"Send me the address I'm about to pull up on you."

"Just type in Dawkins Street. I'll see you! Be looking for the fiends!" I told him before we hung up.

Chapter Twenty-eight
- Bandanna

I had hit my nigga while Precious was in the shower, and I was glad I did. I had been wondering why all day she wasn't trying to let me call him. Talking about she just wanted it to be us. the bitch could've just kept it real with a nigga and we could've still did us. It wasn't like I was trying to wife her or nothing so it wouldn't have been a problem for real. I had a trick for her ass though. I couldn't lie though, because the pussy was fire. We both had been popping Yoppa's all day yesterday and them shit had us fucking like Pitbulls in heat. I had been thrashing that bitch so good, that I had a rug burns on the side of my dick.

Once Precious got her ass out the shower, I offered to take her to get some breakfast. It took her twenty minutes to get dressed and to do something with her hair. She wasn't no dime piece but she was a nice six though. The ass was kind of phat, so it make up for what she lacked in the face. Once we walked outside, I inhaled the early morning air and then blew it back out. Pretty soon it would be getting back cold and I wouldn't wait. I favored the cooler seasons over the hot one's because It gave me a chance to get dumb fresh. The coats, the hats, the boots, and all that shit came out then.

Hitting the lock on the new rental I had just gotten, I allowed us access to the interior. I changed the challenger out for one n them new Dodge Charger's because it had gotten old to me and I was tired of have to let my seat up when I rode more than two deep. That was rare but it added to my list of reasons why I needed to get something else. Scrolling through my phone, I found the new Kevin Gates album and let it play. Once I had my music right, I sped off and jumped in traffic. Precious lived by Central University so I knew I had to take Fayetteville Street almost all the way to Liberty for me to get to Tater Bread. My nigga Yella had put me up on that spot and every time I found myself in Durham early like this, I always made sure I stopped through to snatch me a plate.

Pulling up, I parked and hopped out with Precious after I cracked the window so I wouldn't lock myself out. I left the charger running whit the music going crazy because I always saw Yella do the same thing. I wasn't copying his swag though because in my city I would do the same. I don't know what it is you just gotta be a real hood ass nigga to understand it.

After I ordered out food, I stood by the door and waited as Precious sat in one of the only two chairs the place had to offer. Tater Bread wasn't a sit down spot. It was a walk in or call in and get you shit and go type of place. The food was always on point though and I always ordered the same thing. Cheese eggs, grits, bacon, sausage, salmon cakes, toast, and a big ass lemonade. That's the same thing Yella always ordered to which is where I had stolen the idea from.

We didn't have to wait long either. So, after I grabbed a couple packs of salt, pepper, butter, and jelly we left. Before I jumped back in traffic, I typed Dawkins Street into the GPS on my phone, and it told me that I was five minutes away. As soon as I turned the corner, I saw straight fiends like my nigga told me I would. I saw his as before he saw me because he wasn't expecting me to be in the Charger.

As soon as I saw him, I pulled over and parked behind a big ass black Dodge Ram that was setting to the side. That's when I realized I didn't see the Benz or the Challenger that he had. Looking at the back window of the Ram I peeped a rental car sticker and laughed because this nigga was always in something big. His ass had tricked the shit out me this time though because he didn't even post no picture of him in it on Facebook.

"Yeah, nigga, you slipping!" I said dropping the window once I saw him looking my way. His ass probably thought it was the polce or something because of the tint.

"Wassup, nigga!" He said smiling as he made his way in my direction. I looked over at Precious and she was looking sick. Bitch knew she was about to get exposed.

"Lord, ugh!" She said all dramatic and shit like she hated my nigga or something.

"What's wrong with you?" I asked her with a frown, but I was really trying not to laugh.

"What up, nigga?" Yella asked leaning on the window seal before I could get a answer out of her.

"Oh shit, what up, Precious?" he said as he looked and noticed her sitting in the passenger seat. That bitch ain't even say nothing back. She just kept sitting there eating like she was hard of hearing.

"Oh, you know her, brah?" I asked him smirking as he smirked back because both of us was on out bullshit right then.

"Yeah, she know me, brah, but it's all good though!" Yella said basically telling me that it wasn't nothing

"You still be having the pills, though?" He said looking her way and now all of a sudden, the bitch wasn't deaf no more.

"Yeah, I still got them!" She said looking at him smiling. I guess she was glad he ain't put her on blast in front of me. She just didn't know that I already knew what was up.

"What the hundred pack going for? Still four fifty?" He asked as he started thumbing through a dumb stack of chicken.

"Yeah, but since you know my baby Ill give it to you for four flat!"

"Yo baby? Who yo baby?" Yella asked her but looked at me smirking. He was carrying on ban with it right then for real.

"Bandanna my baby!" She said looking at him and then me and then the inside of her Michael Kors bag where she kept her product. Once I knew she wasn't looking I looked at Yella and shook my head to tell him no the fuck she wasn't. That bitch was tripping if she thought our situation was more than what it was more than what it was. I had already putting her number on the block list in my phone and as soon as I dropped her dumb ass off I was blocking her page next.

"Here you go! I threw you an extra ten too!" She said reaching across my lap to hand Yella the pills. She had them all inside of a small zip lock sandwich bag.

"That's what's up! I'm still gonna tell my nigga I fucked you though!" He said laughing as he tossed her the four hundred dollars. If looks could kill Yella's ass would be dead as hell.

"Word, brah?" I asked playing along like I ain't already know that the bitch was a straight up lair.

"Yeah, man she done fucked me and my nigga ant and now you. That bitch done been around my whole circle man." he said laughing. He was going off with it now, so I found myself laughing along with him. I guess she wouldn't take it because next thing I knew she threw the door open and fling her food out before she jumped out behind it.

"Good, I wasn't trying take that bitch home anyway!" I said turning the car off so I could hop out and chill with my nigga while I ate my food.

Chapter Twenty-nine
– Jakia

That nigga Yella fucked me so good I woke up posting heart emojis on his Facebook wall. He had posted a picture of himself and some dark skinned nigga with dreads. They was up there showing off flashing money and dripping in jewelry like they were superstars of something. I was on that nigga line. I could care less about his bitch because from what I could see she did not look better than me. Shit the way that nigga had me cumming, EJ could get the fuck on somewhere too.

After our sex session, I had laid down on the couch and was out. I didn't wake up until almost two. I had ten missed calls from EJ and one from my sister. I didn't even bother to call EJ back, but I didn't hit my big sis though. That bitch went to Atlanta with some nigga she had just met so I wanted to make sure that she was good.

"Wassup, bitch?" She answered sounding happy as hell for some reason. It wasn't no telling with her ass though because she stayed on ten all the time.

"Shit! Wassup?" I asked back to see if she was gonna tell me why she sounded like the cat who ate the canary.

"Girl, let me tell you! This nigga got that bread! he done took me shopping and he bought me some grills!"

"I'm gonna put them shit in my mouth and wear them! What the hell you think? You acting slow right now for real. What's wrong with you?" She asked screaming through the damn phone. She was so turned I had to hold the phone away my ear because she had my ear drum itching.

"Ain't none wrong with me I'm good!" I told her once I had put the phone back to my face.

"Don't sound like it, but I was just calling to check on you. Did you get some dick last night or nah?"

"Did I?" I asked laughing which made her ask more questions.

"Oh, you and EJ finally made up, huh?" She asked me and I quickly burst her bubble.

"EJ?? Nah, fuck him! I finally got my hands on that nigga Yella!" I admitted with a smile on my face as flashes of our time together played in my head.

"Ooh, bitch, hell nah?" she screamed like she ain't believe me, but I knew that she did because she knew that I never lied on my pussy.

"Hell yeah, and that nigga a fucking animal too. That muthafucka had me bent up all kind of ways in here!" I told her as I got up to fix me something to drink.

"Oh shit! He wasn't doing it like that was he? Let's find out! I might have to try that out when I get back!" That bitch said laughing but i ain't see nothing funny. That bitch was tripping now.

"Nah, bitch, you ain't trying nothing I'm claiming that!" I told that bitch straight up like I just knew the nigga was mine of something. Truth be told, I knew the nigga had a girl so that meant me and him would never be nothing more than fuck buddies. Still, whatever it was that we had or didn't have I wasn't trying to share it with my sister. She already had a handful of niggas she was dealing with so that bitch didn't need mine too.

"Damn, okay! My bad! Better not let ya boyfriend find out" She said laughing through the phone as it beeped. Looking at the screen I saw that it was EJ beeping in.

"Speaking of lame, he calling me now!" I said getting irritated out the gate.

"Aight, well call me later! I should be back tomorrow!"

"Aight, be safe and don't come back pregnant!" I joked before I clicked over to see what the fuck that nigga wanted.

Chapter Thirty
- Keisha

I hadn't seen or talked to Yella since the night I gave his ass some of this pussy. We had been texting back and forth a couple times but every time I tried to get his ass to pull up, he always claimed he was busy. I wasn't feeling that shit and I was horny as hell so that only made it worse. Then my grandmother told me that JC's mother had called to tell her that JC and his baby mama had both been found shot to death. That was my cousin and all, but we weren't really that close, so I didn't even cry when I heard the news. Call me cold hearted or whatever, but I just wasn't one of them emotional bitches.

I went to the funeral, though. Both of their caskets were closed so I didn't get to see what they looked like. I guess they looked fucked up though since the funeral director deprived us who attended the pleasure of see them off. That had been almost a week ago and now here I was stalking Yella's page to see what I could see. That was when I saw that him and Bandanna had taken a picture and posted it. The picture was nice, but my attention wasn't on them. I was looking at the street sign that was behind them. Using one of the phone features, I zoomed in on the sign and read what it said. Two minutes later I was out the door and inside the rented Hyundai Elantra that I had been driving since he day before the funeral. My Malibu was in the shop, so my insurance company had paid for it.

You can call me a stalker, but I really wanted to see Yella. We had only fucked one time but that's all it took for me though. I always fell in love real easy but this time I was on some more shit, for real. I was speeding to get to where my GPS was leading me because I didn't want to miss my chance to see my future baby daddy.

I didn't know how he was gonna act when he saw me, but I was damn sure about to find out. It took me twenty minutes to make it down 70 and through the east to the South Side. As soon as I made the left on Dawkins, my eyes landed on Yella. I already knew what his bitch look like. Ugh! I didn't see her out there though, so I pulled over and blew the horn to get his attention. He did a double take before shock and then confusion set into his face. And then he started walking my way. I hurried up and turned my GPS of as he neared and then I put all my focus back on him.

"What the fuck? What you doing over here?" He asked me a soon as he got the driver side window. He was looking at me kind of crazy which is the same way I was feeling.

"I was coming from dropping my nephew off at the head start up the street and I saw you, so I came back around to pull up on you." I lied with a straight face and a smile. That nigga probably thought I was undercover, and I felt like it the way I had tracked his ass down.

"Oh, yeah?" He said as he looked down between my legs that I had sitting open on purpose. I had on some skintight Versace leggings that stuck to my shape like a tattoo. So, I knew he could see my phat ass pussy pushing through the fabric.

"Yeah! What you up to though? You got time for a quickie?' I asked seductively opening my legs wider as I pinched and rubbed my nipples.

"What? Yo ass crazy as hell!" he told me, but I already knew that.

"Yeah, but you ain't answer my question though!" I persisted because I really needed to feel him up inside me. I wasn't taking no for a answer either and I really didn't want to cause a scene so I was hoping he cooperated with the program.

Chapter Thirty-one
– Yella

That little ho was crazy as hell. That bitch was a stone cold nut, and I knew it. Yet and I was sitting in the passenger seat while she rode my dick. We were in the park parked in the cut on the next street over fogging the windows up as Money Bagz came through the speakers raping about side bitches. I wasn't worried about Shannon looking for me because I had rented one of the rooms in one of the rooming houses for her to boom out of. I felt like it was best if he stayed out of sight as much as possible while CeeCee played the block and brought the customers to her.

I watched the faces that Keisha was making as the matching sounds escaped through her mouth. I could tell that she was enjoying herself because the river between her legs was the evidence that proved it. Back an forth, up and down, round an round she went as she worked herself and used my dick to make herself cum. Once she had accomplished her mission for the third time, I grabbed her around the waist and used my strength to lift an spin and trade places with her. Now she was in the seat with her legs wrapped around my waist as I stretched my legs out and stood in it. I was in a rush and on a couple pills, so I showed no mercy as I fucked her hard and fast making the car rock as if it were dancing to the music it played. Her pussy was making a mess as it leaked and made a puddle on the leather seat. It smelled like straight pussy and Dolce and Gabbana inside the car as the air blew trying its best to cool us down. Yet, I was still seating, and she was still begging for more like she was in heat. I had given her all that I could give her though because I left a shot of protein in her guts fifteen minutes later.

"Goddamn, you ain't no god, yo!" I told that bitch as I pulled out and allowed her to crawl from under me. Back in the driver seat, she ain't do nothing but smile as she pulled her leggings back on followed by the pair of Louis Vuitton sneakers she had been wearing with no socks. Five minutes later she was dropping me back off on the block.

"Don't make me come find ya ass next time!" She said out the window as she pulled off. I watched her go and shook my head.

"I was about to peel out on ya ass. You riding around cup caking and shit!" My nigga Bandz joked as he hopped out the lime green Charger he was pushing. It was the Daytona edition with the Hemi in it.

"Don't hate on a pimp, my nigga. My girl ain't sneak around here, did she?" I asked hoping like hell she hadn't come being nosey.

"Now you know if she had come and ain't see you the muthafuckin sky would have fell. Get the fuck out of here. Yo bitch a real gangsta for real, so you know she would've been on some shit." Bandanna carried on.

"Bruh, she is crazy, huh?" I asked him laughing along with his ass.

"You know, nigga!" He replied simply still laughing.

"Yeah, but look you tryna ride with me and her to go check this spot out?"

"Oh, y'all finally getting a crib?"

"Yeah, I'm tired of that hotel shit. I'm getting a little too big not to have somewhere to kick back at. I'm getting camera's and all that shit and only a few muthafuckas gonna know where it's at, ya feel me?" I said knowing he did because he had been trying to talk me into getting my own shit.

"Say less! But I'm driving the truck. You can push the Charger!" He said giving me the key. I ain't argue with him though because I wanted to see how that bitch rode anyway.

After I slid through and snatched bae, we headed to the address to meet the owner who was a retired banker. The house sat far away from the road and was semi hidden by six feet high bushes that had been trimmed by professional Landscapers. the owner informed us that they come and do the yard twice a month and that we would have to pay for it. I shot that idea down quick because I could give a couple fiends a few dimes to do the same thing. Why pay three hundred twice a month when I could give out five or six dimes? Once we had that part straight, we went on the inside to have a look. there were four bathrooms, a kitchen that connected to the dining room, two bathrooms, a basement and a patio with a big ass back yard.

"And how much would it cost to purchase the house?" I asked the owner to see what he would say.

"Well, seeing as how it sits on an acre and a half, I would have to add that fact to the mix as well as location and I'd say around sixty to seventy - five thousand!" He told me which wasn't all that bad. I thought he was gonna say something outrageous.

"What if I gave you twenty and paid you installments for like five or ten grand every couple of months?" I asked him fishing to see if he was willing to fuck with me.

"Depends! See, the IRS keeps an eye out for things of that nature, so the money would have to be legit!" He replied with a raised eyebrow as if he just knew I was into some illegal shit.

"Right! So, ain't no way around it, huh?" I kept inquiring causing Shannon to look at me crazy until I waved her off.

"I didn't say that!" He quickly said. "I could do what you said and take it and once you've paid in full just make it look like I signed the property over to you! But you might not trust me to do it that way." He added looking at me for a reaction. I didn't say nothing right away because I was trying to see if I could detect any bullshit in his eyes. The eyes never lied and his were telling me that I needed to jump on this train before I missed it. Twenty stacks was a nice chunk out of my stash, but it was gonna pay off on the long run.

"Okay, look! If I do want to do it that way and I give you the money, when can we move in?" I asked, wanting to know.

"Man, the house is ready now. You can move in when you're ready!" He told me and to me he seemed anxious like he really needed the money.

"Okay, give me an hour and I'll be back with the twenty!" I told him before my nigga broke into the conversation.

"Nah, go head get them keys, bruh! I got that in the car. You can just give it back when you get it my nigga. you know how we do!" He told me before he left out to go grab the money.

"Well, I guess I ain't gotta go nowhere then!" I said shrugging with a smile as Shannon wrapped her arms around me and laid her head on my chest.

"Guess not!" The owner shot back as he laughed with delight.

"Why you getting rid of it, though!" I just had to ask him because my curiosity was getting to me.

"Too much on my plate, man. I got other bills and habits to tend to." He explained catching my attention when he said the word habits. Me and Shannon both looked at each other at the same time before I looked back at him.

"What kinda habits you got?" I asked him. Instead of him saying it though, he just took his thumb and flicked his nose. I knew exactly what he meant though, but before I could say anything else Bandanna was coming back in with the money in his hand.

"You got the keys yet?" He asked me after he handed the man two ten thousand dollar stacks that were individually banded. One stack contained blue faces and the other held fifties.

"He does now!" The owner said happily as he handed me two sets of keys that were all labeled. there were three keys on each one for the front, back, and the side door. I gave a set to Shannon, and I put the other one in my pocket before I motioned for the owner to step off to the side with me.

"Just so you know, I get plenty of that!" I told him as I mimicked what he had done with his thumb.

"Is it good, though? I need good quality stuff. None of that trash that has God knows what in it!" He told me making me laugh. He had changed his whole persona now. He wasn't the straight talk proper speaking dude he had been when we first got there. talking about that coke had caused his skirt to come all the way off.

"I tell you what! Give us a few days to get settled and then I'll call you so you can come and see me." I told him because I needed time to throw something together. I didn't have what he needed but I could get it.

"That's fine. Take your time and enjoy the house!" He said as he shook my hand and then waved to my nigga and Shannon before he left.

We left a few minutes later after he did and jumped in traffic. Bandanna was on his way back to Raleigh and we were on our way to Rooms-2-Go. It took us a half hour to cut across town to 15-501 and another two hours to pick out what furniture we wanted. This was my first house, so I went ahead and cashed out. I got beds for each bedroom, a living room set, a dining room set, kitchen appliances, another living room set for the basement as well as a pool table. I paid for it all with cash and told them to deliver it the next day.

After we left there, we went to Wal-Mart and bought cleaning supplies, towels, comforter sets, and six big ass flatscreens for each bedroom, the living room, and the basement. I as planning on the basement being the spot where we entertained our company. The last place we went was my mom's crib so I could snatch up that little money I had stashed there and to grab the Lexus. I didn't even bother to go inside because I knew she wasn't there. My mother drove a XS and it wasn't in the driveway so i knew that she was out and about in traffic somewhere. She was probably running around for my little brothers and sister. It wasn't no telling with her because she was always into something. I had gotten that gangsta shit from my daddy, but my hustle came from her.

Sliding off, I sped in the Lexus while bae followed in the truck. I hadn't drove it in a minute, so it felt strange to me. Me and the Lexus had been through some shit together.

I had made a lot of plays in it which is why it was hot, but I had a trick for that too. As soon as I got everything else, I had going on situated I was gonna leave it parked behind the crib. I wasn't trying to have the police or nobody else stumbling across the crib because they peeped the car. Bay didn't know it yet, but the Lexus was about to be hers.

Chapter Thirty-two
- Yella

The next morning, I was up early even though we had come in late. We ran out of work, so we didn't really have a choice. It was all good though because I needed the rest. Now that I had gotten it out of the way I could get my grind on nonstop. As soon as we got dressed, I started loading our shit in the truck because I wasn't planning on coming back. I was done with the hotel shit unless I was creeping with a bitch. While we were on the way to the house, I hit the plug to place my order. It was after nine, so I knew he was up.

"Yo, what up?" He answered.

"Yo, it's Yella, my nigga!" I told him announcing myself.

"I already know! What it's looking like?"

"I need to see you!" I stressed to him as I bent a right on South Alston to take the back way to 98.

"What you talking about?"

"I got yo chicken and I need a whole dinner, my nigga!" I told him talking in code knowing he knew the lingo.

"A whole dinner?" He asked like he wouldn't believe it or something.

"Big bruh, I ain't playing with this shit! I told you that!" I said smiling because a few months earlier I had been a half gram copping as nigga. Now I was getting a whole thing and running my section while trying to take over some more shit.

"Aight! Aight! Check this out, ya heard? You remember the first time we did anything you came to that spot in the PT?" He asked me.

"Yeah, you want me to pull up there?"

"Yeah, and make sure you solo! No homeboys and not ya girl either." He told me, which had me a little skeptical, but I wasn't sweating it. I never crossed the nigga, so I ain't have shit to be worried about.

"Aight I'm on traffic now! I'm gonna drop my girl off and shoot yo way so give me like thirty minutes." I told him before we hung up.

"Bae, he sound like he about to bless you!" Shannon said looking at me from the passenger seat with a serious expression on her face.

"Why you say that?" I wanted to know because I never did tell her that he had fronted me a whole half a bird so I was curious to know how she figured that.

"I don't know, just my woman's intuition! Plus everything else been falling our way so. But I don't know I just talking." She said as I swung a left into our driveway.

After I helped her take all the stuff in the house except for the bag with the re-up money in it. I ran back outside and tore out. As I drove, I was thinking about what my baby had said. Shit was definitely going good for a nigga.

I knew shit could get greater, so I was about to turn shit up a couple notches. I still wasn't trying to fuck with niggas as far as selling weight, but I had an idea in my mind that I knew was about to fuck the city up. In less than twenty minutes I was sliding through the PT and pulling up to holla at my plug. I knew that the spot wasn't his crib because he was too smart for that. He might have trusted me but I knew that a nigga like him wouldn't sleeping the same place that he sat in.

"What's good, little bruh?" He greeted me after opening the door. I didn't even get the chance to knock because before I got all the way up the steps he was already waiting on a nigga.

"Same shit, my nigga!" I told him as we dapped up. Nodding his head like he knew what I was saying, he backed up and let me in. I had never been inside before because he served me in the driveway the other time I had come. The inside was lace though. It didn't look like a trap house at all, so I figured it was just somewhere he did business at. Once he closed the door, he led the way to the kitchen where a fold up table with matching chairs sat. Now it was looking like a trap house because there were a couple scales, boxes of bags, a money counter, and a few bricks sitting on the kitchen counter.

"That for me?" He asked causing me to look his way. I had gotten stuck when I saw all that white but hearing his voice had brought me back.

"Yeah! It's all there too!" I told him smirking thinking about the last time.

"I hope so! Have a seat while I run this shit through the counter!" He told me before he took a seat at the table. Once we were both seated, he reached for the money counter and placed it on the table. I watched as he ran every single bill through the machine until the digital display showed the total. My count had been right just like I knew it would be. Once he was finished, he sat back and stared at me across the table. I guess he was trying to read me or something. I wasn't tripping though because I had been got used to the weird ass shit this nigga did.

"So, what you tryna do?" He finally asked after having watched me for two whole minutes. He threw me off though because I was trying to figure out what he was asking. I had already told him what I wanted so I was a little confused now.

"What you mean?" I asked to get a better understanding of where he was coming from with it.

"I mean like what you tryna do? What you tryna get out this shit?"

"I'm tryna get paid and run that bag up. I wanna live like a boss!" I answered truthfully because that's what I was really trying to do.

"A boss, huh? How long you planning on staying in this shit?" He asked me as his phone rang. He didn't even look to see who it was before he declined the call. He had three of them sitting side by side on the table and all of them had different color cases.

"I don't see me quitting no time soon, bruh, to be honest. But I ain't tryna bee greedy about it either though." I said and then paused before I continued. "I guess until I feel comfortable enough to stop and not have to worry about nothing!" I added truthfully causing him to nod before he picked up where I had left off.

"Lil bruh, I like you. I mean like I done watched you grind all the way up in a couple months. You know how to get that cash, for real. But don't let this shit take you down!" He stressed to me before he got up before he got up and left the kitchen. It took him close to five minutes to come back. When he did though, he had a Finish

Line shopping bag in his hand that he placed on the table in front of me.

At first, I thought it was some shoes because I could see that two Jordan shoe boxes lay inside. That was until he told me to open the bag and check it out. When I did, that's when I saw that each box held three bricks a piece and it made my eyes light up.

"What's up? I asked him looking up to find him still standing there looking down at me.

"You tell me! Can you handle that?" he wanted to know.

"Hell yeah!" I said without hesitation. who the fuck in they right mind gonna turn down six bricks. Once was already paid for so that meant that five was on front.

"You sure? Cause once you walk out the door that's yo shit!" He said and I knew what he was asking me now.

"Man, I ain't no snitch! I'm gonna make this shit happen!" I assured him with confidence. I had been waiting on an opportunity like that and it wasn't no way I was gonna let it slip through my fingers. Not when I knew that shit only got better from there.

Chapter Thirty-three
- Yella

A month later, I had damn near the whole city going crazy. I still wasn't fucking with no niggas but iI did put my bro in the loop. It was only right because I know he had shit going on up the highway. I knew that he fucked with the soft, so I dropped that raw in his lap and let him get his shine on. I still hadn't caught the nigga EJ, but I wasn't worried about him. I had my little nigga Mils on it because his girl was EJs cousin so it would be easier for him to slide up on the nigga. Worse come to worse if he couldn't handle it then I eventually would. I had other shit to tend to, so I was trying to share the load.

I doubled back around and went back through Bay Creek to fuck with ole girl and I was glad I did. Come to find out her and her sister wee slinging that flake out there but the shit they had wasn't all that. I saw an opportunity and took that shit. Now I was throwing them the soft and their door was getting beat down. I had just pulled off from picking up some money from them when my phone rang.

"Yo?" I answered after recognizing Fran's number. I had her at the Carolina Duke full time, and we had showed that bitch up too. I done went crazy with the work because I was selling weight to the fiend which was cutting everybody's throat. I was slinging grams for forty-five and I wasn't selling no blow up either. I was selling them muthafuckas that gas and they were running back like Mike Vick. I was killing they ass because niggas was trying to dime them to death. I was giving that shit away damn near and it had a lot of muthafuckas in they feelings.

"Yella, I just got robbed!" Fran screamed through the phone causing my mood to change instantly. Shit had been going really good up until then.

"Fuck you mean you got robbed?" I asked but I was already speeding her way.

"They came in here and took everything. They didn't get the money though because I had it in a Ziplock bag in the toilet. They ain't even have no gun they fucking strong armed me, Yella!"

"Say less I'm about to pull up!" I said before I hung up in her ear. I knew she wasn't lying because the day before I had seen some nigga's upstairs sweating us when I had pulled up to get her right. I had seen the itch in them nigga's eyes then but I ain't pay it too much attention. I was willing to bet my last that it had been them sucka ass niggas. It didn't take me but a few minutes to get to the hotel because it was right around the corner from Bay Creek Apartments.

As soon as I pulled up, I noticed the same two niggas standing upstairs leaning on the railing the same way they had been doing the day before. The only difference today was that instead of mugging me, they were smiling. Them niggas must've thought I was pussy or something. It was all good though because I had something for they ass. I had to check on my aunt Fran and replace what had been taken. Business was business and it still had to go on after the smoke cleared. Fran must've been looking out the window because as soon as I hopped out, she came out crying.

"Man, Yella these people are so lucky I'm not the same!" She claimed as she wrapped her arms around me for comfort. I knew she wasn't lying when she had said it though because she had done eleven years for stabbing a muthafucka over forty times. When she went away, I was just a young nigga on the block and in the way. Back then I was still playing with fourteen grams of weed thinking I was hustling. Times changed, though!

"Were they masked up?" I asked wanting to know because I was still betting it was the nigga's upstairs.

"Yeah, but one had on a yellow shirt and the other one had on a red one!" She said describing the same exact things that the two lames had on. Now that she had come out, they went in. It wasn't no need in trying to hide though because I was about to show them how I got down.

"Here, take this and go inside and shut it down until tomorrow, you hear me?" I don't care how much a muthafucka got!" I told her as I handed her fifty-six grams.

"What about the money I got in the room already?" She asked me still crying as I turned to get my strap out the truck.

"Throw it in the truck! I'm about to run upstairs right quick!" I told her as I headed towards the stairwell to go up. It didn't take me no time to reach the top and even less time to get to the room that the two niggas had been standing in front of. I used the XD to knock on the door and then I used my finger to cover the peep hole. Standing to the side so that I couldn't be seen from the window either, I waited. It took a minute, but somebody finally opened the door, and I didn't wait to get invited in. I threw the fire in the first muthafucka face I saw.

"Back up, muthafucka! Nobody fucking move or I'm gonna paint the walls in this bitch!" I promised as I made eye contact with everybody in the room. It was exactly four of them. the two nigga's and two bitches. I recognized the hos but I didn't give a fuck about none of that. I wanted my shit back of I was about to cut the fuck up

"Oh, my good Yella, what you doing?" One of the hos asked me. I could tell the bitch was shook. I think her name was Starasia, but I wasn't sure.

"Man, fuck all that, where my shit at?" I asked before I smacked the nigga I had the gun to. That chrome split his shit on impact and left a gash above his right eye.

"Argh, shit!"

"Shut the fuck up, nigga!" I told his bitch ass as I hit his ass again.

This time, I made his ass fall and then I started stomping his ass as soon as he hit the carpet. I went to the other nigga next, but I didn't touch him.

"Where my shit?" I asked again.

"Y'all got his shit? What he talking about?" The other bitch asked. I know her name was Takera because I used to fuck with the bitch. She was the same one who introduced me to JC and Taylor. I heard through the grapevine that the hoe was on that food and some more shit now. I really ain't care though because she wasn't my responsibility no more.

"Them niggas know what the fuck going on! And that's my word Takera you better not have nothing to do with it I swear to god." I said through gritted teeth because I was starting to get impatient.

"Nigga, I don't even know what's going on so you can miss me with all that extra shit, for real! She shot back with an attitude like I gave a fuck.

"Bitch, shut the fuck up before I pop yo thot ass!" I warned her before I started smacking the other nigga like I did the first. "Now, where my goddamn shit? I'm not asking no more. Next sound I'm gonna make gonna be this fire going off. I'm all the way with this shit if you can't tell by now!" I added and then smacked him one more time just cause.

"Man, it's in the refrigerator, goddamn!" He confessed through bloody lips as he started to cry. the other nigga was still sleep on the floor. I had the right mind to wake his ass up with a bullet to the knee but I ain't want to cause no scene.

"Go get that shit, nigga!" I ordered his bitch as as I smacked him again. I ain't use the gun this time though. I made my palm connect with the back of his head. While he went to retrieve my shit, I used the sheet to wipe the specs of blood off my gun. My first thought when I had come upstairs was to kill them nigga's. The two bitches threw a wrench in my plan though because I knew I would have to kill they asses too. Once I had my shit back, I started backing towards the door that still stood wide open. I knew the nigga's ain't have no strap because they wouldn't have strong armed Fran if they did. I wasn't taking chances.

"Ey yo, check this shit out. Y'all muthafuckas need to get from around here. I come back and y'all still here I'm gonna catch a couple bodies and that's on everything!" I promised nodding my head.

"Where the fuck I'm supposed to go, Yella? I live here!" Takera told me in a pleading voice. Now the bitch know how to talk with some sense.

"Bitch, I wasn't talking to you, so shut the fuck up!" I fired back quickly.

The only reason I was showing her a little love was because the head used to be straight when I used to fuck with her. Her grandmother loved me to death so I couldn't do her like that. Them niggas, though, I'd fire they ass up like a nigga do a Newport fresh out of jail.

Chapter Thirty-four
- Mils

I had been trying to catch up with this nigga for the last few weeks, but he was proving to be hard to find. That was until he pulled up to the Big Apple and I just so happened to be posted up in the front. He was pushing an older model Maxima and I knew it had to be a crack rental because he was a bus rider. I watched as the nigga got out looking the dumbest in some bummy shit. This nigga had to know that he was out of his league. He should've just tucked his tail but instead he had to let his little nuts drop.

"What's up, nigga?" I asked him with a smile that was as fake as a pair of forty dollar air forces.

"Oh shit, what's up, Mustafa!" EJ calling me by my government name.

I hated that name which is why I made muthafuckas call me Mils.

"Shit! Tryna find some gas." I told him throwing the bait because I knew he was a broke ass pothead.

"Word up? My nigga got that official tissue up the street." He let it be known before he quickly added. "And I can get you a deal cuz it's me!"

"Who car you got?" I asked out of curiosity.

"This lil flipper both I been fucking with; she ain't talking about shit though. That how a straight dub my nigga, for real." He told me laughing and I laughed along with him.

I was playing me role real good. It was now or never because I was tired of Yella asking me if I had seen this nigga. I needed to get shit done because the way Yella was throwing coke around, I wasn't trying to put myself on the shit list no time soon.

"What happened with you and Jakia?" I asked but I already knew what was up because Yella had that bitch coin backflips for his ass. Still though, I wanted to see what the nigga EJ was going to say.

"Oh man, fuck that bitch! She acting brand new right now cuz she getting a lil money and shit. I was thinking about robbing her thot ass, but I know she gonna put the law on me!"

"Yeah, you can believe that!" I told him but in my mind I was really thinking if he did that the law would be the last thing he would have to be worried about.

"Yeah, but fuck that ho! Let me run in here right quick and then I'll shoot you to my nigga crib. You smoking with a nigga, right? He wanted to know.

"Come on, you know I'm gonna twist up, my nigga. you driving to so we can ride and blow!" I assured him before he went into the store. he didn't need to know my rental was parked right beside the car he had pulled up in. I waited until he was inside before I slipped the key remote out to secure the doors on the new Lincoln jeep I was pushing.

A couple minutes later, we were shooting up Holloway towards Aston Avenue. His nigga lived in a little apartment on a small street named Peachtree. I gave him two twenties to go and grab a ball of some shit his boy had. Five minutes later we were on the move again. After I had rolled up and we were smoking, I told him to shoot me to Southgate Street so I could make a play. Once we got to Southgate, I had him pull over and then I hopped out as I secretly used my shirt too open the door. I bumped it with my hip to close it back once I got out. Walking around to the driver's side. I motioned for him to lower his window.

"What's good, bruh?" He asked as he nodded his head to the music playing in the car.

"Ey I need you to hold something right quick!" I told him as I looked around.

"Give it here, I got you!" he offered without any hesitation.

"Aight!" I said as I looked back at him and whipped out a blue steel nine.

Before he could reach or react, I was already pulling the trigger. I shot his ass twice in the side of the head before I hit him six or seven times in the chest. Satisfied, I took off running back towards the store that was only a few blocks away.

Chapter Thirty-five
- Yella

I had just pulled up to the crib when Mils hit me about that nigga EJ. To be real, he didn't have to die because ever since I had shot his man and aired all they ass out, he hadn't even been back to the block. Still though, better safe than sorry and that little nigga catch me lacking. I wasn't planning on staying at the crib long. I had just pulled up to change clothes and throw my jewelry on. I was going to Club Diva's with Bandanna to see that nigga Lucci perform. Shit was about to be it for real.

Jumping out the Chevy, I walked to the side door and let myself in. I don't know why I didn't like using the front door. I had been decked the spot out and I had camera's all around the outside and a mean ass security system that sent alerts to my phone. I could even see what my camera's saw without even being at home. Technology was a muthafucka, but it came in handy.

I knew that Shannon wasn't there because I had just left her on Linwood with CeeCee. I didn't have to stand on Dawkins no more because everybody knew to go to Linwood. With the way I was slinging that shit, I didn't have to worry about the fiends around there calling nobody else but me or my girl. I even had Mils pulling up on muthafuckas now. Shit was definitely doing what it was supposed to be doing and that money was stacking up. I had already saw the plug again and I got the same thing as last time.

Once I had gotten dressed in all white from head to toe, I was ready to go. I still hadn't painted the Lexus, but the Chevy was white on white sitting on a lift with eight's up under it. The inside was the same color with yellow stitching and had my name in the headrests. Ever since I had pulled it out the rims shop, I had been pushing it. I let Shannon have the rental and she downgraded to one of the new Camaros.

Back on traffic, I shot straight to the highway because I wasn't trying to be late and fuck around and miss my nigga performing. I had that big four fifty four wide open as I did the dash while sipping on a four. I had started fucking with the lean kind of heavy because there was a draught in the city on the pills. I wasn't tripping though because Bando was dibbling and dabbling, and he had the pint on deck now. Hear him tell it, that bank shit was on pause because the Feds were cracking down in Raleigh. I had offered the coke, but he didn't want that. Then a week later he popped up at my house with a truck full of boxes. Each box held a hundred pints and he had ten boxes.

It took me under thirty minutes to get to Diva's and the parking lot was already packed. I wasn't tripping though because I knew V.I.P. parking had some five hundred dollar spaces open for a nigga like me. Bandanna had already called me and told me that he had paid for my spot, so I was able to back my shit straight in. It was bitches everywhere I looked. It was mid-September so the temperature in the evenings had started to get colder. That didn't stop them hoes from coming out with next to nothing on. One bitch in particular caught my attention right away because she had on a see through dress that only concealed the spots where her nipples, pussy, and ass crack say. I could still tell what she was working with though. That ho was thick and bad as fuck, and I could see that she had come to get chose.

Bandanna met me at the door and after one of the bouncers stamped my hand, he waved me through. I didn't have to wait in line because when you paid for the parking you also paid your way in. Inside the spot was thick and I could smell tree in the air. Once we got to the bar, I saw that my nigga hadn't come by himself because Finesse was waiting along with two other bitches and Bando's little homie Tep. All of us wearing white so it set us apart from everybody else off top. I had on four chains and Bandanna had two. Tep only had on a little one, but it was all good because I had been there. I had learned to never look down on a muthafucka. The same muthafuckas you shit on on the way up is the same ones you gonna need on the way back down.

"Damn, you can't speak?" Finesse started up once I had gotten myself comfortable on a stool.

"Can you? Because I don't remember hearing you say nothing!" I quickly shot back as I took the time to look at her standing there looking like a whole snack.

She had on a white skirt dress with a matching Loui Vuitton heels and enough gold to make a broke nigga wanna rob her.

"Here ya'll go!" Bandanna said laughing as he poured me and him a shot from a bottle of Cîroc that he already had sitting on the bar.

"Nah, I aint tripping about it, my nigga!" I promised before I threw back my shot and then poured myself another.

"I bet you ain't!" Finesse told me before she turned her back on me to watch the crowd.

I'm glad she did because looking at her from behind was a much better view. It had been a minute since I had been in them cheeks and I was thinking to myself that she might can get it tonight.

Bando saw me looking and he shook his head. I knew he knew what I was thinking. Right after that the same bitch I saw with the see through dress walked up to the bar a few feet away and took a seat. She was eyeing a real nigga and I was eyeing her back. Neither one of us made a move though, because before I could they announced that Lucci was about to come out and do his thing. Everybody was on their feet and trying to get as close to the stage as possible. It was more bitches in the spot then nigga's but that's how a club is supposed to be.

Lucci didn't stay up there long though. His performance lasted a little over thirty minutes and then he was gone. It was all good though because at least he showed his face. I wasn't salty about it because this was my second time seeing the nigga. Diva's had a little smoke section outside in the back and I found myself out there smoking a cigarette when the bitch in the see through dress walked up on me.

"What's up with you? She asked me as she invaded my personal space.

She smelled like Chanel 5, and now that she was that close, I could see her eyes were the same color as mine. I usually didn't go for light skinned hoe's but this bitch could get it. She reminded me of that bitch Cubana Lust.

"Shit!" I simply replied to see where she would go next with it. She had stepped to me so obviously she had some kind of intentions.

"Mhm! So, what's your name?" She persisted as she openly checked a nigga out.

Licking her lips, she took her hand and grabbed ahold of the chains around my neck so she could examine them.

"My name Yella! You like jewelry, huh?" I questioned after she had let my shit go with a satisfied smirk on her face.

"Yeah, I like jewelry, but I was just making sure it was real. You know some niggas be fronting and shit!"

"I don't do no fronting! Nice try, wrong guy!" I flexed causing her to let out a giggle. She was eyeing a nigga like she was trying to get into something, and I was with whatever.

"I see that! What you doing when you leave though?" She asked me as she stared into my eyes. I could tell she was trying to fuck and the way her body was looking in that dress had me on the same shit.

"It depends!" I told her.

"Depends on what?" She asked cocking her head to the side.

"Depends on if you leaving with me or not?" I threw it out there boldly because it wasn't no need in playing with the shit. It was obvious that we both wanted to fuck.

"And if I am leaving with you?" She asked stepping a little closer.

"Then we fucking!" I assured her as I reached around with both hands to feel that ass. That muthafucka was pillow soft too and I couldn't wait to see what it looked like out that dress.

All that shit came to a standstill though when I heard a bitch scream back inside the club. Me and ole girl both went to see what was going on and that's when I saw my nigga and Finesse fighting three other niggas'. Tep wasn't nowhere in sight, but I was. it took me zero point two seconds to make my way through the crowd and into the action. I grabbed the same bottle we had been drinking out of and I smacked the closest nigga to me. I finished him off quick and then I went to help Finesse. She had been holding her own, but

I evened it out when I came up and stole the nigga in the back of the head. He didn't fall but he was drunk though so I hit him two more times before Finesse caught him with a mean to piece of her own.

Once he hit the floor, I did him like I did his boy while Finesse went to help Bando. By the time security got to us, we were already finished and ready to go.

Chapter Thirty-six
- Yella

I ended up fucking the shit out of Finesse in the Waffle House parking lot the night before. Now I was pulling up on Canal Street in North Durham to serve one of my plays. I really didn't like coming through this side because the niggas over here were on some other shit. Even though my nigga Bandanna was a Blood, I still didn't get along with the ones that were in my city. Both of my brothers were Crip and I myself had ties with the GDs, so shit wasn't sweet. That's the main reason I had my fire in my lap with one in the head. As soon as I parked, I saw that all eyes were on me. them niggas knew who I was even though I was sitting behind tinted windows. I wasn't hiding though because as I waited for my play to come out, I cracked a rello and then opened my door to dump the guts. My ice started dancing from the sunlight and I peeped the envy on their faces right before I shut my door back. I had just lit my shit when my driver was yanked open. I didn't hesitate though. I had been jumped off the stoop a long time ago so I was TTG.

"Fuck you got going on?" I asked aggressively as I threw the fire in the person's face before I realized who it was.

"Oh, word? You gonna smoke your own buzzin?"

"Almost you running round here playing! What up though?" I said relaxing after I saw that it was my little cousin Heavy. He got the name because he was a little short stocky nigga with a big head. I knew he was blood, but I never knew he hung out on Canal.

"Shit! What you doing over here? You know you ain't supposed to be round here!' He said smirking like shit was funny.

"Nigga, I go wherever the fuck I feel like going!" I told his ass straight up. I said it loud enough so his little home boys could hear it to.

"Man, don't shoot the messenger!" He said still joking as he raised his hands up as if he was surrendering.

"Well, show me who sent the message so I can shoot they ass!" I told him as I looked past him to the crowd of bloods that stood in the driveway across the street behind him. Canal Street was long but it wasn't wide so I know that they could hear our whole conversation word for word.

"Nah, bruh, chill, it's all good! I was just fucking with you. Know nothing popping off as long as I'm right here. We family, nigga!" He said seriously which made me relax. "I was tryna holla at you about something, though!" He added after he saw that I was back calm.

"Well, jump in on the other side right quick then!" I told him.

Once he had moved to do what I asked, I gave the other nigga's a long hard stare just because I knew some fuck shit had been said. I wasn't no dummy, so I knew off top what it was. I wasn't thinking about them lame ass nigga's though because I had money on my mind. Long story short, before I pulled off, I had promised Heavy that I would put him on. It was all good because I didn't like pulling up over that bitch anyway.

I bent a few blocks before I ended up in Bay Creek at Jakia's crib. She answered the door like she usually did wearing booty shorts and a sports bra. Her sister was there also wearing damn near the same outfit. They both looked almost identical except her sister was just a little bit thicker with slugs in her mouth. I was used to being around them though, so it didn't really affect me. Her sister was all the way out with it though and she let it be known that I could get it. Today I found myself sitting between them on the couch a I watched them bag up the coke I had them pumping. I wasn't clocking them because I didn't trust them. I just found it sexy to which two bad ass bitches busting down work. Call me slow or whatever but I liked what I liked. I grew tired of watching what they were doing though, and I started reflecting on other shit.

Ever since I started getting them bricks it seemed like I had a lot more time on my hands. I had the East, part of the South, and now the I had Heavy in the North. I didn't have to worry about the west end because Rontay was all through there. Shannon had Linwood on smash and wasn't nobody trying to buck. It almost seemed too good to be true and deep down I knew that it was. I couldn't put my finger on it, but I knew that a storm was coming. I felt it brewing!

"Why you so quiet?" Jakia's sister asked me snapping me out of my zone.

Her name was Loyalty, but that bitch wasn't loyal to shit but herself. I know this because she was willing to snake her sister on a nigga's line offering me the pussy.

"I'm just thinking about some shit!" I replied as I looked her in the face. Just like always she was giving me that look.

"I hear you!" She said waving me off.

No sooner than she had done that the front door flew open and four nigga's spilled into the apartment.

"Don't do it, muthafucka!" One of them yelled as he ran up on me.

Shit happened so fast that I was slow on the up. Realizing that I had been caught slipping, I ain't even try to buck because it was pointless.

"Fuck ya'll niggas want?" I asked heatedly like I didn't already know. It was a whole nine ounces of soft on the table, and I was sitting there dripping in almost a hundred thousand dollars' worth of jewelry.

"Nigga, stop playing! You know what it is so beat them pockets!" the one that ran up on me said. The other three were busy grabbing the work and keeping their eyes on the two sisters.

"Man!" was all I could say because my pistol was on the fucking table out of my reach.

"Man nothing! You got three seconds to give that shit up or I'm shooting and I'm still gonna get it when you dead!!" he threatened me. Bitch ass nigga was tough as hell right then, but he had the upper hand.

"You right!" I said nodding as I emptied my pockets and gave that nigga everything I had.

"The jewelry too, nigga!"

"Fuck!" I said as I started taking my shit off. They threw everything in the same bag that I had brought the work in. Once they were satisfied, they started backing out one by one until the last one made it through the door. As soon as he did, I reached under the couch and grabbed the drake that I had left there. Every spot that I chilled in I had put something big there for times like these. It paid to be prepared and I was about to cash in. I ran to the door and thew the choppa over the rail spraying shit. The first nigga I hit was the one that held the bag. The second one caught it because he was trying to turn back and grab the bag. The last two took the hint after seeing their people get dropped but I still wasn't letting up. Niggas had me fucked up, for real. They got lucky though because I ran out of bullets. Once that happened, I ran back to the apartment door.

"Yo, ya'll don't fucking know me, right?" I yelled at the two sisters. I knew the niggas came for they ass and I just so happened to be there.

"Boy, go head, get out of here you good we got you!" Loyalty assured me cool as a fan. Jakia on the other hand was crying like a baby. I didn't have time to comfort her though because I had to get the fuck on. On my way down the stairs, I kept my head down in case somebody was peeping out their window. I snatched up the bag with my shit in it on my way down and kept it moving. A minute later, I was tearing out in the Chevy.

Chapter Thirty-seven
- Loyalty

The police had come knocking, but we hadn't seen shit and don't know shit. Fuck them nigga's because truth be told I knew they had really come for us. That shit was crazy as hell though. Yella was retarded as hell but that gangsta shit made my pussy wet. My sister was doing the most with all that crying shit. It was a good thing that the shit happened during the day because most of my neighbors had been at work. I still couldn't believe Jakia's dumbass had left the fucking door unlocked. I was glad that Yella had been here though because ain't no telling what would've happened. Shit could've definitely went way left but instead it went so right!

Business was still doing what it should. Me and Jakia still had two ounces in the freezer that we were just sitting on. We weren't letting muthafuckas come to the apartment though because the police were still running around trying to figure out what happened. That's why after they had knocked on the door, I made Jakia get dressed so we could go ahead and get the fuck away from there for a little while. We waited long enough for the police to move the bodies and then we moved right behind the coroner's van. I had a little pink on pink Audi A4 with my name painted on the hood in black cursive letters.

"Yo, you really need to tighten the fuck up. You doing the most right now lil sis and you gonna fuck around and make this nigga nervous!" I told my sister because she was still shedding tears over muthafuckas that had come to do her harm and tried to take money out her pocket. I was having a hard time understanding where she was coming from with all the emotional shit.

I had to get her right because I knew, sooner or later, Yella was gonna be calling trying to holla at us about what went down. I wasn't trying to die because this little bitch was gonna fold. I know her ass had never been in a situation before, but I had so I know that a murder was the easiest thing to get away with. The police didn't suspect us anyway, so she was crying for nothing. I wasn't gonna let her mood spoil the rest of my day though. there was still money to be made and I planned on getting it.

Chapter Thirty-eight
- Yella

I drove straight to the Carolina Duke because it was the closest place I could think of where I could sit my ass down and think or a second. I had already called Bay so she could come get me and of course she had a thousand and one questions for a nigga, but I banged in her ear off top. I didn't have time for all that because I needed to clear my head and figure out what to do from there. I knew that nobody had seen my face because all of Loyalty and Jakia's neighbors worked during the day. I was more or less worried about them talking and the other two fools that had gotten away.

"Nah, them hos ain't gonna fold!" I told myself as I knocked on Fran's room door. I had the bag of work and the drako in my hand looking hot as shit.

"Boy, what the hell you doing with that?" She asked me as I pushed past her as soon as she had opened the door. She was looking at me like I was crazy, but I wasn't stunting her ass because that's how I felt.

"Nothing! Nothing!" I answered as I sat down on one of the two beds that were in the room. That's when I noticed that there were three other people in the room.

"Ya'll gotta get the fuck out!" I told them as I laid the empty choppa beside me.

"Boy, you don't be coming up in here putting my company out!" My aunt Fran fussed, but I wasn't trying to hear that shit.

"Fran, look now! Don't play with me right now cuz it ain't time for all that shit. Just do what the fuck I said!" I flexed angrily as I started to roll me a blunt. Lord knows I needed to smoke bad as hell. I didn't have to tell her twice because she knew when I was serious.

"Okay! Okay, y'all gotta go just come back later!" She told them as she ushered them out of the door. Once they were gone, she closed the door and then come and stood directly in front of me.

"Now, tell me what the fuck?" She asked me as she looked down at me with a frown.

"Man, I just had to kill two niggas!" I told her heatedly because I knew I could trust her with my life. She knew about a lot more than that and it had never leaked through her lips so I wasn't uncomfortable talking to her.

"Boy, why the hell you keep killing people children?" She fussed before she walked off to grab herself a cigarette from the box that rested on the nightstand.

"Man, them niggas ran up in one of my spots and tried to rob me. Ain't nobody taking nothing from me or my people I don't give a fuck!" I told her ass straight up and I meant that shit.

"Police looking for you?" she asked puffing on her cigarette.

"Nah, I don't think so!"

"Well, what you gonna do?"

"I'm gonna go drop the Chevy off at the shop and I'm gonna keep doing me. I need you to do something with this though!" I told her as I patted the drake.

"What you want me to do with it?" She asked scrunching up her face like she smelled shit or something.

"Fuck you think, Fran? Get rid of the muthafucka! Wait until the sun go down though and bury the muthafucka behind the hotel." I instructed as a horn blew outside. I knew it was my baby without having to look so I jumped up and opened the door.

"Don't forget what I said!" I threw over my shoulder before I slammed the door.

Outside, I made Shannon jump in the Chevy while I took the Camaro. I made her follow me to the paint shop down Roxboro Road where we left it. Once I had the Chevy, I climbed over the arm rest and let her drive. I guess she felt the vibe because she didn't bother me as I smoked me another blunt. We were passing by a small car lot when I peeped a fresh ass 745 with a reasonable price tag in the window. That bitch was all black and tinted out with some black and chrome shoes on it.

"Turn around, bae, and pull up at that car lot!" I told Shannon as I pointed behind us. She didn't ask no questions and an hour later I was speeding through the city in a foreign. I still owed fifteen thousand on it, but I was pushing it like it was already paid for. If it wasn't for the IRS, it would have been. The first place I went to was back through Bay Creek to see what it looked like. The police were still out there but I saw that Loyalty's Audi was missing so I hit her line. When she answered I told her to pull up at the Red Roof on North Point Drive. It was a street over from the Carolina Duke and a couple blocks away from the crib. It took her about fifteen minutes to pull up and I let her circle the parking lot a couple times to make sure I wasn't being set up. Once I was absolutely sure I called her and told her what I was driving and where I was parked.

"So, what's up?" She asked as she looked at me after she had jumped in. I didn't detect any fuck shit in her eyes, but I still wasn't convinced.

"Where yo sis at?" I asked because she was nowhere to be found. I couldn't see through the tint on her car so I didn't know if she was in there, still at the apartment, or what.

"She in the car! She on some little girl shit right now but I got her!" She assured me as I looked at her.

"Damn, that shit was crazy as fuck yo!" I said looking away from her to look out my window.

"It's gonna be okay, you aight!" I heard her say as I felt her hand park itself on my thigh. When I didn't say anything, I felt it moving up further until it reached my zipper. After that it was inside my jeans. That's when I looked at her and saw she was biting her lip as she stared at me.

"What you are doing, Loyalty?" I asked like I didn't already know.

"Showing you that you ain't gotta worry about us! It's still the same as it was before that shit happened!" She promised pulling my dick through the hole in my pants. Before I could protest or stop her, she was climbing across the armrest and sliding my dick into her pussy. I hadn't had the Beamer a whole hour, and I was already fucking something in it. I don't know if it was the fact that her sister was waiting in her car two spaces away or if her pussy was just that good, but I didn't last nothing but ten minutes. I knew she had got hers too, though, because unlike her sister, she was a screamer.

Chapter Thirty-nine
- Jakia

I didn't care what my sister was talking about because that shit had scared the fuck out of me. I had been around plenty of guns and had done shot them muthafuckas too. I hadn't never been robbed though and then to be that close to a murder, it was just a lot to take in at on time. I was okay after a while though because Yella had gotten us a room at the Red Roof or two weeks. He also had given my sister the money for us to go shopping so we didn't have to go back to our apartment for anything to wear. I never did see him, but my sister did, so she relayed the message to me. Now her ass was in the shower singing and I was laying on one of the beds flipping through channels on the TV. I was trying to see if that shit had made the news. Once I saw that it didn't, I relaxed and turned the TV to VH1.

I don't know why, but as I laid there I started to think about EJ. I had heard about him getting killed a few nights before and I couldn't do shit but shake my head. That nigga had always been in some shit and I had always known that it would eventually catch up to him. Now he was gone, and I was recollecting on our relationship and the times we had. It was what it was and what it wasn't it never would b because he and us were now a memory. Even though Yella wasn't my man, he filled a gap that I didn't even know I know existed. Not to mention that me and Loyalty had made more money in a month fucking with him then we had in the whole six months that we had been hustling.

Loyalty and I had been stripping until we got tired of that and decided to take money we had saved and invested it in a pack. It didn't take us long to take off because we were serving all the stripper we knew and a few off brand niggas. From there our clientele grew and it was still growing. Now Yella was talking about finding us a plug on the pills and right when shit was looking good it went all to hell because of some nigga's that didn't want to see two bitches shine. I was glad Yella had been there with us for real. His ass deserved some good slow head for that shit.

"Fuck is you smiling at?" My sister said snapping me out of my thoughts as she walked past ass naked. I couldn't help but to check out the artwork she had going up her leg to her butt cheek. I remembered the day she had got that shit.

"Nothing, just was thinking about something!" I told her taking my eyes off her and focusing back on the TV.

"I'm glad you back because I was starting to think you was gonna have a nervous breakdown or something!" She said as I saw her putting on lotion.

"Nah, I'm good now." I assured because I was.

"Good cuz that shit over and done. As long as we aight you shouldn't worry. But we definitely gotta move because I ain't comfortable going back living there!" Loyalty said and I couldn't do shit but agree because I felt the same way.

Chapter Forty
- Fran

I felt like a damn fool sneaking around at four in the morning. I had to keep my baby safe though, so I was doing what needed to be done. I went to Ace Hardware and bought a shovel and everything. It took me twenty minutes to dig a grave for that big ass gun. Once I was done and I felt the hole was deep enough, I threw it n the hole and covered it up. I had already wiped it down with bleach and wrapped it in a hotel towel before I came out. Once I was done, I took the shovel and threw it in the dumpster on my way back to my room. I had made all my company get out while I was gone because I couldn't leave them in the room alone. Not when I had Yella's shit and his money in there. Hell to the nah! I was aunt Fran but even I could get my ass whooped if shit came up missing and I ain't know where it was at.

"Damn, you took long enough! It's cold as shit out here, Fran!" Harold said as I walked up. Harold wasn't nobody special, but he had been spending money all night, so I didn't curse him out.

"Don't worry about what I got going on!" I said as I unlocked the door and went inside. He was right behind me no doubt ready to take a blast.

"Where everybody else go?" I asked once I had taken a seat on the bed.

"I sent them to the store!" He answered as he came and stood in front of me with lust in his eyes. I knew what he wanted but I wasn't doing shit until I loaded my stem and took me a blast. Once I had done that and left earth in my spaceship, I yanked Harold's pants down.

"Yeah, baby, I like it rough!" He told me as I took his preschool erection in my hand and guided it to my mouth. I knew that it would be over real fast because he was half of a minute man. I could put his whole dick in my mouth and still have room left over for my food. I guess some people just weren't blessed in the grown man department. As soon as he came, I took me another blast and watched as he took his. I loved smoking crack because there was just something about feeling my soul leave my body. It was a euphoric feeling that I couldn't explain. A person would have to smoke some to understand where I was coming from.

I heard knocking at the door, so I jumped up and went to the door. Looking out the peep hole I saw that it was my company, so I let them in. NeeNee, Tasha, and Rhonda strolled in with eyes so wide open that they looked like owls. It wasn't no mistaking it because they looked like zombies and I told them that!

"Y'all hos is gone somewhere for real!" I said laughing my ass off because the new shit Yella had dropped on me was some fire.

"Mmh mhm!" That was all NeeNee could say because her mouth was locked.

Chapter Forty-one
- Yella

It had been a week since I killed them niggas. I wasn't tripping though because it was what it was. Catching a body wasn't nothing new but me letting a witness live was. Especially when they was outside my circle. I didn't feel it in they vibe though and Loyalty was a whole hundred so I knew that i could trust them. I was laying dick to both them hos and it had me tripping off how bold that bitch Loyalty was. She had rode my dick like a real porn star while her sister was a couple feet away. That shit was wild, but it was all good though.

That was then, now me and Bandanna were cutting through South Carolina on our way to Atlanta. I was riding shogun while he drove. I had a drako stashed under the backseat along with a forty and Bando's FN. We also had eighty thousand between the two of us, so we were low-key riding dirty. We were still Blowing that tree though as if we weren't already sitting up high enough in this big ass Silverado Bands had rented for the trip. We were on our way to ATL because there was still a drought in the city on the pills. Word was there wasn't any molly floating around either. I couldn't say if the molly part was true or not, but I knew for a fact that it wasn't no yuppa's around. I was about to change all that though.

Bandanna's baby momma lived in Atlanta, and she swore that she could get us as many pills as we wanted for a dollar a pill. As soon as I heard it, I was with it because I could make ten times what I spent being that the price was ten apiece in Durham. I was gonna do it just like I did the coke when I had started though and sling them shits for three for twenty. A muthafucka couldn't beat it because they we quadruple stacks. It took us seven hours to hit the city and we went through and scooped up his baby mama as soon as we touched. We weren't there to play so it was business first and then the strip club after. After she led us through the city to some neighborhood called Summerhill, we pulled over and parked. It looked like we were in the hood, so I grabbed my gun out the gate and threw my nigga his. We didn't get out right away because we had to wait for her to tell the nigga that we outside. Five minutes later dude walked up to the truck and Bandanna's baby mama got out to holla at him. after they had their little words, she signaled for us to get out as well.

"What's good, shawty?" He asked speaking to Band's first. The nigga was an average looking dude with dreads that hung past his shoulders. He was definitely dripping, though, with a big ass diamond necklace around his neck that had an iced out pill bottle as the pendent.

"Shit! Came to fuck with you and spend some money!" Bandanna replied nodding as they dapped up before dude turned my way. I had been sitting back sizing his ass up trying to read him for any signs of fuckery.

"What's up with you?" He asked me holding his hand out.

"Ain't none!" I told him keeping it short and sweet as I accepted his outstretched hand. Once all the introductions were done, we followed him to his place of business and got a chance to see the merchandise. This nigga didn't just have the ex, he had perk 30s and the oxy 30s, and molly capsules. I knew for a fact that I could sell the perks and the oxys for twenty-five apiece which was a huge flip. Me and Bandanna ended up both spending forty thousand each. we had money in our pockets to go ahead and cash out, but we still had to eat, pay for gas, and I wasn't leaving until I hit the strip club. I popped one of the ex-pills before we left to see what it was hitting for. I had gotten a variety of them that included Instagram's, Transformers, and The Incredible Hulk. All of them were quadruple stacks so I only took a fourth of a piece. By the time we had dropped off his baby mama and reached the hotel where we were staying, I was lit like a torch.

After we put everything in the room it was close to ten o'clock, so we went right back out and headed to Magic City. I hadn't never seen so many bad bitches in one place in my whole life. I'm talking about short, tall, brown, black, yellow, red, white and I even saw a purple bitch. She had her skin painted as part of hr outfit with an ass so phat it couldn't have been real.

"Look at ya! You dirty dog! Put ya tongue back in ya mouth, Beethoven!" My nigga told me as we made our way to our booth. We were following behind a bad bitch who was leading us here. I didn't know if she dance or not but that ass was jumping in the skimpy outfit she had on.

"Nah, nigga, I ain't Beethoven, I'm Chico! I'm gonna bite one of these hos!" I said and I was dead serious because a couple hours later I was doing just that. Me and Bando had left with two bad ass bitches. Shit wasn't free but it was worth it though. we had took them hoes back to the room and trashed they ass North Carolina style. The bitch I had was thick as shit and I was on them beans. So, when I had turned the hoe over to hit it from the back I bent down and bit that bitch. I didn't do it hard enough to draw blood, but it was enough to make her ask me to do it again. that's when I bit the other cheek right before I jumped back in the pussy.

Me and Bands didn't even go to sleep. We stayed up fucking with them hoes until we left them in the room and jumped back on the highway. We left as soon as the sun started coming up at six and we were pulling in my driveway a half hour past two. As soon as Bandanna left, I was right behind him after I had put most of the pills up. They were already bagged up by a thousand per bag, so I took three bags with me. One was ex, one perks, and the other was the oxys. I had a twenty thousand ex pills altogether and then ten thousand each of the other two. I was about to fuck the city up for real. I was going to fuck it up quietly though because I was gonna let Jakia and Loyalty handle the hand to hand. That's why I was pulling up at the Red Roof now. I didn't even call them to let them know I was coming because I wanted to pop up. I had my own key to their room, so I let myself in and found them both sitting on the bed smoking a blunt. I could tell that I had surprised them, but I really fucked them up when I pulled the pills out of my bookbag.

"Damn! Oh shit that's what the fuck I'm talking about!" Loyalty shouted jumping up doing a dance like she was in the music video. That bitch was thrown off. Her and her sister were like night and day. While Loyalty stayed turned up and, in the mix, Jakia was kind of quiet and really a good girl on the low.

"How many pills is that?" Jakia asked as she reached to pick up one of the Ziplock freezer bags.

"It's a thousand in each bag. The yappa's going three for twenty and the perks and oxys is going twenty a pop!" I explained as both of them listened. I could've set the price for the perks and the oxys at twenty-five and thirty but I was trying to go ahead and get the shit off fast so I could re-up. It wasn't no need to be greedy because I was gonna see my money back plus a lot more. I was guaranteed to make at last close to a ticket minus what I would have to cut out to pay them. I couldn't lose!

Once I had them straight, I jumped right back in traffic to go around and check my trap. My first stop was Linwood though, because I needed to see my bitch and make sure she was in the right place. I never told her that I was coming right back so I know she thought that I was still out of town. As soon as i bent the block I peeped the Lexus outside the rooming house. It was black on black now just like my Beamer. As soon as I pulled up, CeeCee came and jumped in the car trying to talk my head off. I could tell she was high as a kite because her eyes were wide open. After I got her to finally shut up I sent her inside to go get my baby. Five minutes later I saw Shannon come out the door wearing all black like he was me or something. I could tell she had a gun in her hoodie because the pocket on the front was hanging low from the weight.

"Hey bae!" She sang before giving me a kiss after she had jumped in the car.

"What's up?" I asked leaning back as I relit the blunt I had in the ashtray.

"Nothing! Everything good! How was the trip? You back mighty fast!" She said looking me over before she leaned over to sniff my dick like I was dumb enough to come back home smelling like somebody else.

"Shit, you might as well handle yo business while you down there!" I joked laughing causing myself to choke on the gas I was puffing.

"I can!" She assured me as she started to undo my pants before I stopped her.

"Nah, I'll let you get me right tonight cause yo ass coming home as soon as I finish making my rounds!" I told her straight up because she needed to take a break. I could tell that she hadn't been home when I was there earlier. that meant she had been in the trenches since I left. Shannon had started sleeping in the rooming house and everything. It wasn't a bad thing, but it was time for her to come home and take a break.

"Damn, daddy, tell me what to do then!" She sassed and then pouted like a kid.

"I just did! You riding with me or you gonna drive the Lex home?" I asked with my poker face because wasn't nothing up for discussion. Long story short, I pulled off with her in the passenger seat after she left CeeCee with enough work to get through the night and most of the next day.

Chapter Forty-two
– Rontay

Ever since my brother started throwing me the work, I had been seeing more chicken than Popeye's at the grand opening. I don't know where the fuck he was getting it from, but that shit was fire. I could do whatever I wanted to it. I could blow it up, stretch it, leave it, or whatever! He was only throwing me a nine at a time, but I couldn't complain when I had barely been copping a zip. Now I was using the money I was making off the coke and I was putting it with my dope money to cop a bigger pack. I had Creedmoor going crazy with that food which is why I was pulling up at the BP now to meet somebody. Creedmoor wasn't really a city. It was more like the country with a bunch of long back roads and trailer parks. The trailer parks were like the country version of the projects.

Ten minutes went by, and my play still hadn't pulled in yet, so I jumped out and went in the store to buy me some rello's. As soon as I was about to walk out, I saw four all black trucks speed into the BP parking lot. I knew that it was the law out the gate but what made me almost shit on myself was when they boxed the car in. As soon as I saw that I walked out the store and around to the back where I hit the woods running. I had everything on me already, so I wasn't worried about them finding shit in the car and I had been driving a dope rental, so the car wasn't mine. I was still pissed though because I knew I had been set up to get knocked.

I didn't stop running until I got to the trailer park a couple streets over. I had a little bitch that lived out there, so I ran straight to her crib. Once I was safely inside, I breathed easily. That's when I remembered to turn off my phone. what I really needed to doo though was get the fuck out of Creedmoor, so I made my little bitch take me to Durham. She wanted to chill with me, but I was on some more shit though. I needed to get rid of my phone and I needed to go grab my whip. I wanted to go back and see if I could catch the nigga that set me up slipping, but I wasn't trying to take no chances. Them muthafuckas had pulled up looking too federal and I wasn't trying to see it.

"So, you gonna come through later or nah?" My little bitch asked me before I got out. Her name was Kokita but everybody called her Kita for short.

"I might when I finish handling shit." I lied knowing damn well Creedmoor wasn't gonna see my black ass no time soon. I was done with that town and Butner as well since they were basically the same.

"Aight, just call me and let me know."

"I got you!" I promised as I got out and hopped in my shit. I had left my car in the hood on Briggs because that's where I had been when I rented the car. I had been just about to pull off when I saw a black BMW bend the corner and stop beside me.

"Fuck is this?" I asked myself as I gripped just in case it was an opp.

Chapter Forty-three
– Yella

Me and Shannon ended up going to Olive Garden first. After we ate, I bent through the Carolina Duke and picked up the little money Fran had for me before I hit Mils up. Once I pulled up on him in Hickstown, I shot to Canal Street to fuck with Heavy. I had started him off with a four and a baby to see what he was talking about. The next day he had hit me back for another one, so I upped him to a nine and that' where we were at with it. I shot to the east next and bent a right off Holloway on Briggs. As soon as I slid around the corner, I peeped Rontay getting in his car, so I pulled up on him. That nigga owed me a little change, so I needed to see what was up. Bruh was one of them muthafuckas you had to stay on top of because he liked to play them little kid games with a nigga bread.

"What's up, fool?" I asked after I dropped the window. I knew he didn't know it was me because had just bought the shit I was in. It was so new it still had paper tags on the back where the license plate went. Didn't want too many people know I had this and I wanted to keep it that way.

"Where you get that?" he asked answering my question with one as he leaned out the window to check my shit out.

"I had this shit like a week now!" I told him with a smirk.

"Crack rental?"

"Nah, nigga, this is my shit! You about ready for me though? Cause I just got my hands on an ass full of pills but I ain't fucking with you until you clean up!" I told his ass straight up.

"What kind of pills? He wanted to know but ain't say shit about my money.

"Ex, perks, and oxys and I got a lot of them so tighten up so I can get you right. I told you I was about to turn this shit up!" I told him before I sped off and left him where he was at. I wasn't trying to be sitting for too long because I didn't want to be seen. I had been moving like Casper lately and I needed to stick to the same routine. I bent a right on Lathrop and took it across Guthrie up to Park Avenue. A left then two rights brought me to TeeTee's spot where she was already waiting for me on the sidewalk. just like my brother, she didn't realize it was me until I dropped the window. She didn't make a big deal about it though because she was used to seeing me swerve up in different cars. Just like Rontay, I kept our conversation short and sweet. I grabbed what she had for me and then hit her back with what she needed.

The next stop was the car shop so I could go snatch my baby. I had gotten them to dip it in bright canary yellow, but I left the rag top white. The shoes were painted yellow and white to match the body. The inside already coincided so they didn't have to fuck with the interior. I was glad them fuck niggas had made me kill them because my Chevy was looking way sexier now than it had looked before. I had that Kevin Gates cranking through the system as I swerved through traffic with bae behind me.

Once we made it home, we parked around back like we always did. I was still on the same shit, and I didn't want nobody knowing where I lived. I wasn't worried about nobody trying to pull a kick door because I had that bitch more secure than Fort Knox. I was worried about a nigga talking too much and leading the law to my door which was something that I didn't need.

"Bae, I'm going to take a shower right quick!" Shannon said as soon as we walked through the door.

"Shit, maybe I'm the one that need to be sniffing!" I said jokingly with her because of the move she had pulled earlier.

"Boy bye, I ain't you!" She sassed back with her smart ass mouth.

"That's a fact! It's only one me!" I fired right back not missing a beat as I headed to the basement where the stash was. See when I had bought the pool table it gave me an idea that I had never heard of being done. I had gotten my man's from the car shop to come to my crib and put a stash spot in the table the same way that he did the car's. So, after I pressed the hidden button that was located under the right corner pocket and a second button that rested under the right middle one, the top of the table opened like the hood on an old Corvette. There was only enough space inside for me to hide a hundred bricks at the least. Right now, though, it only held the pill's I had just came up on and four and a half squares. Me and Shannon were the only two that knew about this spot and that's the way I wanted it.

Grabbing one of the bags that held the ecstasy, I stole one pill and then secured the stash. By the time Bay got out the shower I was sitting on the bed ass naked stroking myself. She knew what it was, so I didn't even have to tell her. She walked over still wet from the shower and replaced my hand with her mouth. While she did that, I took the ex pill I popped it in half. I threw half in my mouth, and I made her pause long enough to place the other half on her tongue. I was still lit from the day before, so the half only boosted the way that I was already feeling. I got topped off for thirty straight minutes until I got bored sitting there watching.

That's when I decided to let her up before I made her get into doggy style position. I wasn't ready to fuck yet though. Instead, I snatched her up with my arms around her waist causing us to go into 69. While I stood eating her pussy in the air, she hung upside down and continued where she left off. She didn't know that I had my phone recording us, but I did. I was putting on a show because I planned on watching the video as soon as we were done. Me and bae were both freaks, so we wound up doing some of everything. Our fuck fest went on for two hours before we stopped to take a break. That's when I grabbed my phone and showed Shannon everything that we had just done.

"Ugh, why you do that?" She fussed trying to take my phone out my hand. After a while she gave up and started watching it with me. When it got to the part where we did the 69, she made a noise that sounded like a growl and a moan mixed.

"We gotta do that shit again, for real!" She told me as we kept watching until the video was interrupted because somebody was calling.

"Yo?" I said answering to see who the hell was fucking up my quality time with my girl. Even though she had been against the video at first, I could tell that she had grown content with it because she smacked her teeth when I didn't send whoever to voicemail.

"Where you at, fool?"

"Who's this? Mils?" I asked sitting up because he sounded like he was in trouble. I could hear it in his voice that something was wrong.

Chapter Forty-four
- Mils

I had been fucking around with this little bitch named April from Cornwallis for like a week now. It wasn't nothing serious because I already had a bitch. That hoe had been all n my DM and in my inbox on Facebook, so I finally went on ahead and linked up with her. Long story short, I had been keeping her ass with me ever since because the head was crazy. She had sucked and fucked me the first time we kicked it. The bitch was a straight up dime too, yo! That was the icing on the cake! She had a slim waist, super phat ass, and she looked like a light skinned version of the porn star Cherokee. I guess that's what got me and made me slip.

We bent a right on the strip at the bottom of the projects when she told me to pull up in her parking lot. I wasn't tripping about it because I ain't have nowhere to go at the moment, so I did it. I didn't know that it was a set up the whole time though. I found out real fast but that shit ain't go how muthafuckas thought it was gonna go. As soon as I peeped the play I started shooting until I had backed them niggas up off of me. I know I had hit at least two of them and it had been six in all. Once April saw that her little plan had backfired, she called herself trying to jump out but I quickly snatched her dumb ass back in.

"Nah, bitch, don't leave yet!" I said through gritted teeth because I was on ten, for real. I had shown the little hoe love and she turned around and tried to snake a nigga. I wasn't tripping though because after I had put her brains all over the right side of the car, I felt like we were even.

"Damn!" I mumbled as I backed out and tried to turn around. Realization had set in that I had just fucked the rental up. That was the least of my worries though because as I tried to pull out the projects, the fucking police showed up. I guess somebody had called and gave a description of the car because they tried to block my path. I wasn't going for it though, so I jumped the curb and took they ass on a high speed. I had to because I ain't have no other choice. I was dirty as fuck with a pistol. That was the least of my worries though because I also had this dead ass bitch sitting beside me looking stupid as fuck. I was in a fucked up predicament and I was making it worse by running. Wasn't no way in hell I could just give up though because if I did, I would never see the streets again. I had to at least try to get away.

That's why I called Yella. I had been talking to him when I lost control of the Jeep and smacked a car that had run a red light at the intersection of Fayetteville Street and Lawson Avenue. without missing a beat, I jumped out with everything and took off on foot. I was right in the heart of the North Carolina Central campus. Had it been daytime I could've blended in with the college kids. My luck was running fucked up though, so it was after school hours. Still, I took off in the direction of the campus and I didn't look back.

Chapter Forty-five
– Yella

I was speeding going fast as I could without tearing my shit up or getting myself pulled. I knew that if Mils had taken the police on a high speed chase though, that damn near every coop in the city would be focused on the situation and not me. I had jumped in the 745 because the Chevy would have been too bright and plus, I knew the BMW was way faster. It took me twenty minutes to get to Fayetteville Street and I noticed that the police were everywhere. the farther I rode, the more I saw. Finally, I made it to the intersection where I peeped the Lincoln Jeep that Mils had been driving. That nigga had totaled that shit and I was glad I hadn't used none of my resources to get it. I saw that somebody was still in the Jeep. I knew it wasn't Mils though because whoever it was, was a female and it looked like shawty was dead. She wasn't my concern though, so I sent a quick text to my little nigga's phone and asked him where he was at. He texted back asap and told me that he was coming through the trail that ran between the Burger King and MacDougal Terrace. By the time he got to the end I was already sitting there waiting with my lights off. As soon as he jumped in, I peeled out and flew up Lawson towards Durham Tech.

"Nigga, what the fuck you got going on?" I wanted to know as I turned the music completely off by muting it from the steering wheel.

"Man, this ho tried to set me up, so I had to pop a couple niggas and then I did that bitch too." He explained, still breathing hard from having been on the run for his life.

"You left the bitch in the Jeep?" I asked remembering what I had seen when I was riding past the scene.

"Hell yeah, I shot that bitch in her face! Fuck that bitch, yo!"

"So, how the fuck the police start chasing you? what you was doing? You was speeding or what?" I continued asking questions as I cut across the railroad tracks at the end of Driver Street.

"Nah, them muthafuckas swarmed the projects before I could get up out of there. I ain't have no choice but to take they ass on one. Some dumb ass ran a red light, and I couldn't stop so I smacked they car." He confessed shaking his head.

"Why the hell did you smoke the ho in the rental though?" I asked because I couldn't understand that shit.

"Man, I don't know!"

"You better know something! This shit might blow up in yo face my nigga." I told him knowingly. His prints were all over that rental and he had been to jail before. Once they tracked the person who rented the jeep, it wasn't no question that they were going to tell it.

"I know, man, I know, goddamn!" He said nodding his head as he rocked back and forth in the passenger seat. I knew I would have to think for that nigga. By the morning, they would be looking for his ass and I didn't need him getting caught. I ended up taking him to my crib, so I could keep my eye on him.

"Just chill right here for a second, my nigga! Let me get that cause you don't need it. Most definitely gotta get rid of this!" I told him as I took his gun from him. I left him sitting in the kitchen while I went to the bedroom where Shannon was slipping on a pair of sweatpants.

"Where you going?" I asked her placing the gun on the dresser.

"I ain't going nowhere I was coming to see what's going on?" She said looking at me for an answer. I didn't answer right away because I wanted to shut the door before I started talking.

"Man, this nigga, Mils done fucked up, bae! I might have to get rid of him man cause he know too damn much!" I told her truthfully.

"Get rid of him? What you mean like kill him?" She asked me like she couldn't believe what I was saying.

"First of all, you too damn loud so calm the fuck own! And yeah, I mean kill him! He know too much and I ain't tryna get jammed cause he was being stupid. He done killed some muthafuckas and the police is all over it!" I explained to her, but her face told me that she still didn't get it.

"Okay, so, what does that have to do with you?" She asked.

"Cause, man, me and him done did a lot of shit together and the only way to get of a murder charge is to beat it or snitch about another one!" I said breaking it all the way down to her so she could comprehend where I was coming from.

"You had him with you when you killed Ruga, didn't you?"

"And he was there when Joog got killed!" I revealed but I left out the part about JC and Taylor.

"I knew yo ass did that dumb shit! Man, goddamn, Yella! So, what you gonna do? You can't leave me out hereby myself bae!"She said breaking down. I knew it was the ex-pill fucking with her emotions though, but I needed to think and all he crying shit wasn't gonna help nothing.

"Look, shut the fuck up, aight. I'm not going nowhere! We gonna handle this okay!"

"We? How the fuck WE gonna handle it?" She asked me as she looked at me with the crazy look.

"You love me, right?" I questioned as I stared at her the same way she was looking at me.

"You ain't even gotta ask me that!" She assured me and now instead of looking crazy she was looking like I had offended her. The tears were gone as well and that's how I knew she was high.

"Show me you with me then!" I told her as I grabbed the gun I took from Mils. Once I checked to see that there were some bullets still in it, I handed it to her.

"You want me to shoot him, bae?" She asked me in a hushed voice.

"In the head!" I confirmed with a nod.

"Bae!" She whined.

"You don't love me then!" I said reaching to take the gun back.

"No!" She said shaking her head snatching back so I couldn't take the gun.

"If you need me to do it, I'll do it, bae!" She told me. The next thing I knew I was following her to the kitchen. Mils was sitting with his back to the door and his head buried in his arms.

He didn't even know what was happening and he never would because she put the gun to his head and squeezed the trigger. Once and then a second time. Satisfied, she turned around and looked at me.

"Don't ever question my love or loyalty ever again!" She said before she gave me a kiss on the lips and handed me the gun.

Chapter Forty-six
- Shannon

I don't know how I was supposed to feel after killing somebody. I could honestly say though, that I didn't feel shit. Nothing at all! Not even now as I helped Yella roll the body up in the rug that had been in the living room. We wrapped the body in black garbage bags and taped it up so that the blood wouldn't leak out. Once we had him rolled up, we carried him out to the Chevy because we knew that the BMW trunk would've been too small to try and fit the body in. the plan was for me to follow Yella so that's what I did. I didn't know where we were going, and I didn't care. I just wanted to hurry up and get this shit over with. We drove around until finally we pulled into a subdivision that was still under construction. Choosing a house that had already been completed, we both pulled up and parked.

"Watch out while I go dig this hole!"He told me once he got out and had walked up to the window. I nodded and watched him go. It took him a minute to find a spot and started digging. Once he did though, I timed him as I kept an eye out for trouble. An hour later, he came back, and we pulled Mils out of the trunk. Once we had him in the hole, Yella sent me back to the car to watch out again. He didn't take as long to cover the hole as he did digging it. Once he was done, he came and tapped on the window

"Drive the Chevy cause I got all this dirt on me! I ain't tryna fuck my interior up!" He told me once I had lowered the window. that nigga had to be out his damn mind. We were out there hiding a

236

dead body and his ass was worried about keeping his fucking Chevy clean! I didn't say anything though. I just did what he said to do and then I followed him home. Once we got there, we took a shower together to wash away the evidence of the sin we had committed. I still didn't feel any type of way about the situation. Not then and not even when I got out the shower and cleaned up the mess I had made in the kitchen. I never knew that people's brains wee grey. I always thought they were pink or red like the color of blood. Well, I guess not I knew because I was looking at the proof as I wiped it off of the table and into the trash can. One thing was for sure though, we were definitely getting a new table because I know for a fact that I wouldn't be able to eat off that one.

"You aight?" Yella asked sneaking up on me causing me to jump.

"Yeah, I'm good." I assured him because I was.

"You sure?" He asked turning me around to face him.

"Bae, I'm straight! I promise!" I insisted as he continued to search my eyes while wrapping his arms around me. I was still rolling off the pill, so his touch felt extra good. I guess he could see that I was turned on because my nipples were hard and poking him in the chest. I had been cleaning the kitchen naked and he come looking for me in the same outfit.

"How about we finish what we started earlier?" He suggested as he lowered his hands to grip my ass. Without warning, he picked me up and I wrapped my legs around his back.

"You gonna do that thing you did earlier?" I asked because I really wanted to do that shit again.

"We can do whatever you wanna do!" He promised me before he carried me to the bedroom. After that we didn't talk using words. We had a discussion using our bodies.

Chapter Forty-seven
- Loyalty

It had been six months since Yella had put us on with the pills and life couldn't have been better for us. I had upgraded my car to an Audi truck and my sister bought herself a Mercedes Benz CLA 250. We were backing the strip club again, but it was just a front so that we could push our shit. Between dancing and hustling we were both taking home close to five stacks a night. The bank account was looking lovely. We had moved out of Bay Creek and went across town where we were leasing a house on Cook Road. That's where I was headed because I had to get ready for the trip. When I pulled up, I saw that Jakia was already home. I also saw that Yella was there too because his truck was backed in the driveway in my damn spot. Ever since he had gotten that big muthafucka he had been thinking he was the shit.

I wasn't surprised when I walked in the house and found that he had my sister bent over the couch tearing her ass up. He was fucking, he real good too and I couldn't help myself as I started coming out my clothes. Oh, we were all the way out with it now. It wasn't a secret no more. Me and my sis had come to an understanding that he was both of ours. It was also understood that we belonged to him. We weren't allowed to have boyfriends, but we were cool with our arrangement because he kept us booth satisfied and paid. That's why as soon as I saw my sister's leg's shaking, I made him pull out of her and run up in me! Once I had got mine and he came inside me, I went and got in the shower with my sister. Thirty minutes later we were out and ready to go. We had packed the night before so all we had to do was put our stuff in my truck and go. This was our second time making this trip, so we already knew what to expect.

"Aight, now y'all be safe and do the speed limit!" Yella instructed like we didn't already know this.

"Boy, we good!" I told him as I threw on Gucci shades. He was leaning on the passenger side window where my sister was sitting. She had already kicked off her Gucci sneakers and had her legs curled under her. I knew she'd be asleep before we even got past Charlotte.

"Aight, and don't forget to put that shit in the stash spot before y'all jump back on the highway!" He continued like I hadn't said shit. I couldn't be mad though because he was only trying to make sure we were on point.

"We got you!"Jakia assured him.

"Aight, call me when y'all get there!" He said before he backed up so I could pull off. I already had my phone on YouTube so as soon as I pulled off, I pressed play and let Lucci sing to us.

Chapter Forty-eight
- Yella

Six months can do a lot for a nigga when he on the come up. I had made myself into a boss. I had the pill game on smash and I was the nigga to see for the work. I still didn't like fucking with niggas, but I had gotten a little too big to keep sticking to bust down. That's why I came up with a way to meet myself in the middle. I started serving niggas in third person and I put people in spot to move work for me. I wasn't on the block no more because I had to fell back. My name was ringing too loud in the streets, so I had to be careful nowadays. I had pulled Fran away from Carolina Duke and made her come back to the hood. She wasn't doing no more tricking because she didn't have to. I paid all her bills and she had plenty of crack to smoke. I was hitting my little cousin Heavy with a brick every week now and he had the whole North side doing back flips. he had taken that gang shit and used it to his advantage. As long as he kept the money straight I ain't give a fuck what he did.

TeeTee had fucked around and overdosed and died. The landlord didn't even let a whole month go by before he was trying to rent her shit out. The duplex was in the perfect spot, so I snatched it up and threw Shadai, Muffin, Ginger, Porsha, and all them in there. I had PeeWee and Forest in there too, so it was a hoe house slash trap house. I ran a brick and a half through there every three days. Rontay had finally decided to get with the program, so I had him booming out a spot in the west end. That spot was too federal, so I never pulled up there. I was hitting him with a brick and three thousand pills every week. I knew he could do more, but he was trying to juggle too many drugs at one time so that's what was slowing him down. Shannon was still on Linwood, but I had made her switch the swag up because at the level we were playing at now, I couldn't afford to have her moving reckless.

Nowadays, she was letting CeeCee make all the plays on Linwood, and she had Mitchell running Dawkins. The only thing my baby was doing was supplying them with the work and collecting the money. She also had CeeCee's little boyfriend selling pills and powder for her. Between all of them they ran through two bricks a week. Shit was sweet and anybody looking could tell because I had just bought a new Escalade and it sat on thirties. It was the same color as my Chevy with a system that quaked so hard, a muthafucka could hear me from five or six blocks away.

That's what I was hopping in after I watched Loyalty and Jakia pull off. I had them taking the trip to Atlanta now and this would be their second time going. I don't know how I pulled it off, but I did and I had them hoes wrapped around my finger. Anything I told them to do they did without asking questions. it had been my idea to put them back in the club because I saw the benefit in it. that's how I was able to go to the dealership and pull off the lot in my truck. It was in Loyalty's name and Jakia had co-signed for it.

Pulling off, I slid up Cook Road and bent a right at the light. Hillside high school was on my left until I got to the next light and made a left by the new BP they had just built. I was on my way to meet the plug because he had hit me up saying he wanted to talk. I had just seen him a week before, so I was trying to figure out what he wanted. I didn't have to wonder for long though, because as soon as I pulled up to the Burger King across from Central, I saw that he had beat me there. I left my shit running as I hopped out wearing straight Gucci from head to toe. I had parked beside him so my stroll to his car was short.

"What's up, my nigga? You good?" I asked as soon as I jumped in his car. He wasn't driving the old truck today. He was in the new Jaguar that had just dropped. It was plain jane except for the tint but it was still fresh.

"Yeah, I'm good. You good?" He asked back as he looked at me.

"I'm Gucci!" I answered still trying to figure out what the fuck was up. he was throwing me of and I started to wonder if I was being set up or something. I didn't have shit on me but a gun but still.

"Check this out! I know you wondering why I made you pull up out the blue and shit but I needed to holla at you face to face!" He started and then stopped.

"Holla at me about what?" I wanted to know.

"Remember when I asked you how long you was tryna stay in this shit and what you was tryna get out it?" He asked me. I remembered the conversation real well. It had taken place the same day he had fronted me them first five bricks. I was trying to figure out where he was going with it though, but I guess I was gonna find out.

"Yeah, I remember why what's up?"

"What's up is I done got all I'm gonna get out this shit. Staying in it any longer than this would be considered greed!" He told me and broke my heart all at the same time.

"Nah, man don't tell me that!" I said raising my voice a little because he had sprung this shit on a nigga out the blue.

"I ain't got no choice, lil bruh! Them people watching and I see they ass!" He expressed to me, and I could tell by his voice that he was fucked up about it.

"Who watching you, the Feds?" I asked already knowing that them people had to be the Feds. "Damn and you got me in the car and shit!" I said as I started looking around to see if I could see them.

"Nah, ain't none here cause I shook them." He assured me as he sat there a little too calm for a nigga that was under investigation.

"So, why you make me pull upon you for?" I wanted to know because I was ready to get the fuck on for real. Nigga was hot as a muthafucka and had me around him. I didn't need them flames jumping on me. Not when shit was going good for a nigga.

"You see the car parked next to us?" He asked nodding his head to the left causing me to look. I was expecting to see the feds but instead I saw a low key Honda Accord with some bitch behind the wheel.

"Yeah, what's up with it?"

"I left you something in the trunk. You don't owe me nothing for it. I just want you to run that bag up and fall back!" he told me and then held his fist out for a pound like he always did when he was finished talking.

After we bumped fists, I jumped out and was about to close the door when he stopped me.

"Ey, make sure you wait until I'm gone before y'all pull off. She gonna follow you until you stop but don't drive to the other side of the world cause we gotta hit the highway!" He explained to me, and I nodded in understanding. I did exactly what he said even though I was nervous as hell because the situation was weird. I still felt like I was being set up, but the nigga in me had to see what was in that trunk. So just like a dummy I hopped up in my truck and mashed out with the Honda behind me.

When I didn't go that far though because I knew the Campus Hills community center was right up the street. I drove all the way to the back to make sure we weren't being followed and to keep nosey eyes out of the mix. When I jumped out, I motioned for her to pop the trunk. Once she did, I opened it up and saw that there were three duffle bags laying inside. I had to peep what was inside them because it was only right. When I did, my eye's landed on more coke than I had ever seen in my life. Seeing all that white had me stuck for a minute until realization kicked in and I thought about the fact that I was looking at enough work to put a nigga in prison for life. It took me two trips to unload the bags from the car and carry them to the truck. Once I had grabbed the last bag, I shut the trunk and then patted twice to let her know to pull off. The plug had literally handed me the keys to the city. Now, it was time to turn up for the streets.

The End.

The Ruler of the Red Ruler (By: Kutta)

The Trenches: Murder, Money, Betrayal (By: Kutta)

Block Boyz (By: Juvi)

Da $treets Raised Me & Da Guns Paid Me (By: Juvi &
Splash Queen)

Team Savage (By: Ace Boogie)

Team Savage 2 (By: Ace Boogie)

Team Savage III (By: Ace Boogie)

Love Have Mercy (By: Kordarow Moore)

Love Have Mercy 2 (By: Kordarow Moore)

Rich Pride (By: M.L. Moore)

Hittaz Die Every Day (By: Michael Lawrence)

The Price Of Loyalty Is Death (By: BlackGod)

Available at Bagzofmoneycontent.com and most major bookstores

About The Author

Samuel White aka Blue Hunnid was born and raised in the mean streets of Durham, North Carolina. He is an author, entrepreneur, musician, and a visionary. He started writing books while sitting in prison; he has written fourteen novels. His dream is to become a rap artist and to succeed in reaching his goals. He is currently incarcerated at Edgefield Federal Correctional and is scheduled for release in 2024. His plan is to keep writing in hopes that his stories will generate enough revenue to kick start his music career and other business ventures upon his release. He is also on social media and can be reached at Lit Grymee on Facebook and Instagram or by mail at Samuel White #34448057, PO box 725, Edgefield Federal Correctional Institution, Edgefield SC 29824.